Pop Goes
the
Weasel

Stephen Osborne

Dreamspinner Press

Published by
Dreamspinner Press
5032 Capital Circle SW
Ste 2, PMB# 279
Tallahassee, FL 32305-7886
USA
http://www.dreamspinnerpress.com/

Pop Goes the Weasel

Cover Art by Anne Cain
annecain.art@gmail.com

ISBN: 978-1-61372-677-8

Printed in the United States of America
First Edition
August 2012

eBook edition available
eBook ISBN: 978-1-61372-678-5

Once again, for Matt Downing
for reasons both obvious and obscure

Chapter One

I OPENED one bleary eye.

The world, or what I could see of it, consisted of a round-backed wooden chair upon which most of my clothing was placed, a dresser that had several drawers open, and a nightstand. On the nightstand sat a small clock on which the big hand was on the five and the little hand was on the nine. This seemed to me to be a silly time to rise, so I rolled over, intending to snooze until the clock had the decency to indicate a more reasonable hour, such as noon or one o'clock.

When I rolled over, my nose collided with something hard. A hand. I wiggled the fingers on both my hands. The hand by my nose remained still. Not mine, then. I shifted some bedsheets and uncovered a face. The face was pretty. A young man with long, curly brown hair.

I couldn't remember a thing about him.

I thought. I vaguely recalled attending a party thrown by my friend, Caps. Caps, or Jake Winston, if you wanted to believe his birth certificate, was known as Caps because one year, in a rare fit of generosity, his father had bought him a cabin cruiser. The cruiser didn't last long, as we took it out on spring break and sank the damned thing by running it into a coral reef lurking in a rather ridiculous spot, but we had called him Caps, short for Captain, and the name stuck.

Okay, so, party thrown by Caps. I seemed to remember dancing quite a lot and doing tequila shots with someone. That must have been the brown-haired beauty. I may also have done a sort of striptease on Caps's kitchen table, but no other clues were coming to me.

I closed my eyes. Maybe after a few more hours of rest, my memory would return. I at least wanted to remember if the sex I presumably had with the curly-haired stranger was fun.

No sooner had I snuggled against my pillow, though, than a cacophony of thumps sounded at the door, making my head jerk up. I immediately regretted the action that made the room spin and made my brain feel like an unhappy giant was squeezing my skull.

"Weasel, are you in there?" came a voice from beyond the door. I knew it must be Caps, but in my state the voice seemed to reverberate and boom like a devil in a bad horror movie.

"No," I replied, letting my head drop back to the pillow. "Go away."

Caps, never one of nature's better listeners, opened the door and popped his head inside the room. He had straight black hair and a rather odd face, all cheekbones and no chin to speak of. Somehow the visage came together in a way that didn't scare children and small dogs, but we never exactly figured out how. "Weasel," he said, "your stepmonster's on the phone."

I groaned. That didn't bode well. "Tell him I died." It wasn't far from the truth.

Caps brought the rest of his body—or what there was of it—into the room. I'm on the thin side myself, but Caps was *so* thin that he could double as one of the skeletons they always have hanging around in science classes. "He was pretty insistent."

"He always is." I rose slowly, hoping my head wouldn't roll off my neck onto the floor. It throbbed a bit but stayed attached. I looked over at the beauty lying next to me. He hadn't stirred. "I think this one's dead."

"That's McCaffrey. He's a heavy sleeper, especially when he's had a few."

McCaffrey. Nope, meant nothing to me. Hoping he'd been fun, I tossed the covers aside and slid out of the bed. Things spun around a bit but eventually came to a stop, and I took in my surroundings. I realized I was still in Caps's house, a big place off-campus that he shared with a couple of his buddies. I was in the spare bedroom. I was also naked. I looked down. My erection looked back at me. I looked at Caps. "Oops," I said.

"I've seen you naked before, Weasel. Many times. In fact, sometimes when you enter a room and you've got clothes on, I ask people to introduce me to the stranger who's just come in."

"Funny." I located my underwear on the chair and put it on. One sock was on the chair. The other was under McCaffrey's back. We must have disrobed in a hurry. I yanked the sock out from under him and sat on the bed to put them on. "Why didn't the stepmonster just call my cell phone?"

"He did. You dropped your cell phone into the toilet last night, if you'll remember. It probably isn't working at its best right now."

I had a hazy recollection of fishing my phone out of the bowl and then putting it up to my ear and saying "Can you hear me now?" like that guy in the commercials. It had seemed funny at the time.

I put on my jeans and figured I was clothed enough to face the outside world. I followed Caps downstairs to the kitchen. The phone was on the wall. I picked up the receiver. "Hello?" I said.

"About time you answered, you worthless bag of bones."

For my stepmonster, that was fairly complimentary.

Let me rewind a few years. My father had been dead for several years, having died in a motorcycle wreck. It wasn't actually the wreck that killed him, to be precise. He'd been eating a banana while cruising down the road and went into a slide. The slide itself wasn't of the fatal variety, but he choked on the banana. It was tragic, but in a way fitting. The man really did enjoy his bananas.

Dear old Dad left my mom a pretty sizable hunk of money, and I guess she had trouble spending it all by herself, so she went husband hunting. The crop of husbands must have been thin that season, because she ended up with Jasper K. Dollings, aka Stepmonster.

Dollings not only had money of his own, but he was one of those holier-than-thou types as well. The church he belonged to wasn't that of Fred Phelps, the notorious minister who went around arranging protests at gay funerals, but it was close. Dollings believed that all gays were on the fast track to Hell and should be either sent to brainwashing centers to be cured or put in camps to separate them from "normal" people. My mother begged me, in order to keep some kind of peace in the family, not to let Dollings know that I practiced the "love that dare not speak its name." Not easy for a good-looking, marvelously sexy young thing like me, but for Mother's sake, I keep mum when at home.

I swallowed several pithy and pointed replies and merely said, "And hello to you, too."

Daddy Dollings ignored my comment. "I need you to come by the office this afternoon. There's something I have to go over with you."

I didn't like the sound of that. The last time he asked me to join him for a confab at his office, he wanted me to work part time for him while still attending college. College itself was taking up too much of my free time. I didn't want anything resembling work encroaching on my leisure activities and adventures. I consider myself an amateur adventurer. Not an easy thing to be in Rockford, Illinois, but I manage.

"Not sure I can make it," I told Dollings. "You know, classes and all that."

"Since when have you ever gone to your classes? Be here at two. And don't be late. You've already put me behind this morning by having to track you down. Why the devil don't you answer your blasted cell phone? I had to call three or four of your disreputable friends before finding out where you were."

"My phone sort of took a dive, and water not being on good terms with electronics, it isn't working so hot right now."

I heard the stepmonster sigh heavily. "You're a waste of space. I sincerely hope you grow up soon and stop pretending that you're still in high school. I blame your father for not raising you with more of an iron hand."

I bristled at that. My father may have been fatally fond of bananas, but he was a good sort of guy. I said as much.

Dollings scoffed. "He was a wastrel, and you're a son of a wastrel. All that changes at two, though. See you then." He rang off without so much as a good-bye or even to ask if the scrape I had on my knee was healing properly. The man had an odd sense of Christian values.

While I'd been chatting with Dollings, Caps had been preparing coffee. Now that it was ready, he poured us each a cup. "What was all that about?" he inquired.

I shrugged. "I'm not sure. I'm supposed to meet the spider in his lair at two o'clock. I'll find out then, I suppose."

"He probably wants you to go with him this weekend."

"Doubtful. The stepmonster likes to spend as little time with me as I do with him. Why? Whatever is going on this weekend?"

"I told you last night."

"I can't even remember the guy I woke up with. Anything you said last night can be put into the category of the forgotten." I sipped my coffee. It was strong and helped me wake up but wasn't sweet enough for me. I wandered over to the sugar bowl and began heaping in spoonfuls.

Caps shrugged and began to recap. "My great-aunt Charlotte died."

"Condolences."

"Thank you. Anyway, her will is being read this weekend at her monstrosity of a house out near Shannon."

Understanding began to dawn. Caps's family and my stepmonster were pretty matey, being in the same business, which was publishing books that no one wanted to read. You know the type. Volumes with titles such as *An Exhaustive Treatise on Carpal Tunnel Syndrome* and *Post-pragmatism in Business.* I'd rather read some of my college textbooks than skim over anything published by Dollings Press. Not that I've read any of my textbooks, but you get the idea. Now, if they assigned mysteries in class, I'd be aces. I love reading mysteries.

Knowing that many of the Winston clan worked at Dollings Press or were stockholders, I nodded. "The stepmonster thinks that your great-aunt has left him a bundle, and despite the fact that he's already got plenty of green himself, he wants me to be there when they announce that he's even richer."

Caps made a sour face. I'm not sure if it was the coffee or the conversation. "I've got to be there myself. It won't be a fun weekend. The house is out in the middle of nowhere, and there's nothing to do. I'm glad you'll be there, though. You can help me out."

"You need the Weasel moral support as well? Don't worry, old friend. You'll have it in spades."

Shaking his head, Caps said, "Keep your moral support. I couldn't care less if Charlotte left me a dime. I want you there to build me up in Keith Sutton's eyes."

"This, as Sherlock Holmes used to say, is a new development in the case. Who is this Keith Sutton and why the buildup?"

Caps sighed dreamily. "He's the nurse that stayed with Aunt Charlotte—"

"Great-aunt, you said."

"I usually just call her Aunt Charlotte. Great-aunt is a mouthful. Besides, as a great-aunt, she wasn't that great. Anyway, Sutton stayed with Aunt Charlotte during her illness. He's fantastic. Beautiful. Intelligent. Caring. And gay. But he won't consider going out with me. He thinks I'm rather dim and frivolous."

"You *are* rather dim and frivolous."

"That's where you come in," Caps said, taking no offense at my honest statement. "I need you to point out my good characteristics to him."

"That's not going to be easy. I wasn't aware you had any."

"Be serious for a moment, Weasel. I'm counting on you. This is the man of my dreams. We were meant to be together. He's perfect for me. I just need to get him to see that. And whatever you do, don't steal him."

I thought this was a low blow, especially since we'd agreed never to bring up the John Adair incident again. Recently, Caps had burst into my room to find me and this Adair guy engaged in some sexual acrobatics. I hadn't known at the time that Adair was supposed to be dating Caps. It had caused a rift in our friendship that had lasted weeks and we had only recently mended things. I still felt that I hadn't been at fault, as nowhere on John Adair's body were found the words "Property of Jake Winston." And believe me, I looked everywhere.

Not wanting to dwell on the past, I patted my old friend's shoulder. "Say no more. By the time I'm done with this Sutton, he'll think you're a mixture of Mother Theresa, Gandhi, and Lady Gaga. Maybe a bit more Gaga than Gandhi. He'll be begging you for a date."

Caps set his coffee mug aside and patted my shoulder too. "I knew I could count on you, Weasel."

I think, for those of you who may not be in the know, I ought to point out here that my name isn't actually Weasel. On the birth certificate, the actual reading goes Patrick Carrington Weasley. Yes, Weasley, just like the redheaded brats in the Harry Potter books. My friends tend to go for nicknames, so Weasel was an obvious one for me. My hair, it should be noted, is not red. It's blond as you can get without actually being white, and pretty thick. If I let it get too long, it curls at the ends, especially around the ears, giving me that Princess Leia side-buns look. Luckily that doesn't happen too often.

I returned to the spare bedroom to fetch my shoes. McCaffrey was still snoozing away. I made a fair bit of noise putting my shoes on, hoping he'd rouse himself enough that I could thank him for whatever may have happened during the night, but his snores continued undisturbed. I returned to the kitchen, where Caps was pouring himself another cup of coffee.

"You said you're supposed to meet your stepfather at two?" he asked. "What are you going to do until then? Got any classes today?"

I nodded. "Several." I looked at the clock on the wall. "Right now I'm supposed to be in History, or 'Dead People and Dates', as I like to call it. Then at eleven I've got my Folklore class. I might actually go to that. We're on ghost stories and legends right now. Pretty interesting stuff."

"You can do some research this weekend, then. My aunt's place is supposed to be haunted."

"Really? Some old Winstons hanging around?"

"At least two. There's supposed to be a Gray Lady who haunts the upstairs bedrooms. Those who have seen her say she looks sickly. All pale and thin."

"Being a ghost will do that to you."

"And then there's Great-granddad Winston. He died in World War Two. Supposedly he's seen wandering around the place with half his face blown off."

"Sounds ghastly. Don't you have any sweet, little-kid ghosts or something like that? I'm not sure I want to bump into spectral sick ladies in gray or soldiers minus half a face."

"There may be. It's that type of place. My cousins and I would go there for the Christmas holidays and scare the crap out of each other." Having finished his second cup, Caps tossed the mug into the sink. "Strange your stepmonster wanting you to come along to this Will Party. It's a big house, but he's bound to run into you a lot, and you're always saying how he hates your guts."

"What you say is true. However, my mother has been trying to get him to make an effort to get to know me better. This is probably his idea of spending quality time with me." An idea hit my brain with a jolt, a sign that my foggy head was beginning to clear. "Um… your aunt isn't going to be there, is she? I mean, like, laid out in a coffin in the living room so we can all have a peep? Corpses kind of creep me out."

"No, we chucked her in the ground Saturday. There'll just be me, a bunch of older Winstons, and a few people from Dollings Press, all hoping to be mentioned in the will. And, of course, Keith. I think Charlotte promised him a little reward, so he'll be there. You won't forget, will you? About talking me up to him?"

"He'll grow sick of hearing your good points."

"Good. Because if you fuck this up, you'll be joining the Gray Lady and Granddad Winston."

The threat was delivered in a jocular tone, but I still bristled slightly. "If I'm to be a ghost," I told Caps, "I'm not haunting your aunt's gloomy old place. I'd choose someplace livelier, more fun."

"Such as?"

"A gay bar, of course."

Chapter Two

EVEN though the stepmonster insisted I be on time, I still had to wait for nearly an hour before his secretary announced that I could go in and see him. I think this is standard practice with book publishers. They get some author wanting to see them, all full of themselves because they wrote *An Examination of Passion and Betrayal in The Scarlet Letter*, but after cooling their heels in Jasper K. Dollings's waiting room with only his secretary for company—a woman who looked like she could double for one of the cauldron-stirring sisters in *Macbeth* at a moment's notice—they suddenly are timid creatures who agree to a mere 10 percent royalty when they were holding out for 15. Why he kept me out in the Forbidden Zone I have no idea, since I wasn't one of his bevy of frightened authors. Habit, I suppose.

When I finally was ushered into the inner sanctum, I tried to keep a smile on my face as I approached his desk. That was another trick of his. His office is huge, and his desk is placed at the far end so that the visitor has to trek quite a ways to actually get to my stepfather. By the time they get there, they're worn out and their throat is parched, and they just sink into one of the purposely uncomfortable guest chairs and agree to whatever unreasonable demands Dollings wants just so they can get the whole thing over with and escape. I was fortified with Caps's coffee and a pretty big lunch, though, and I was relatively braced when I sat down opposite him.

The stepmonster eyed my T-shirt and jeans with disfavor, a look meant to wither. I beamed back at him, unwilling to let him intimidate me. I even crossed my legs so that he could get a good look at my scruffy tennis shoes. The look deepened to a scowl. Some people can't scowl, at least not successfully. Jasper K. Dollings was a Master Scowler.

"You look," he said, "like you slept in a sewer."

It was on my lips to tell him that in fact I had slept with someone named McCaffrey and not in a sewer but in Caps's spare bedroom, but I held my tongue. The time would come when I would have to burst my stepmonster's bubble, but not yet. Instead I arched an eyebrow. The best defense against a Master Scowler is to arch an eyebrow at him. Works like those bullet-deflecting bracelets that Wonder Woman wears. "Surely you didn't ask me up to your office to discuss my sleeping habits?"

I could tell he wanted to thunder on a bit, but he swallowed his ire and got down to business. He probably wanted me out of his office as much as I did. "That's true. Actually, I have a favor to ask of you, much as I hate to admit it."

I slouched a little in my chair and pressed my fingers together. "Pray continue," I said.

"Why the hell are you talking like that?"

"I've been reading the works of A. Conan Doyle lately. It's the sort of thing that Sherlock Holmes says to a client when they're beating about the bush and not coming to the point."

"Well, stop it. You sound like an idiot. And if you're not careful, I'll come to the point by kicking you in your skinny ass."

He looked like he'd enjoy it, so I unpressed the fingers and sat up straighter. "Go on."

"Better. Now, one of the board members of Dollings Press, Charlotte Winston, passed away recently."

"That would be the great-aunt of my friend Caps. He was telling me only this morning that she died."

"Who the hell is Caps? What sort of a name is Caps?"

For a religious sort, I noticed that Jasper K. Dollings peppered his speech with a lot of "hells," but I thought it best not to mention it. Instead I filled him in on the nickname. "You'd know him as Jacob Winston. We call him Caps because—"

"I couldn't care less why you and your wastrel friends call him Caps. It's immaterial why you call him Caps. Now, where was I?"

"Jake's Aunt Charlotte has kicked the bucket."

"Oh, yes." The stepmonster did a little swing back and forth in his swivel chair while he chewed on the tip of a pen. "There's to be a reading of her will this weekend at her house out in the country. I've been invited for the weekend, and I'd like you to come with me."

"The comfort of a stepson in a time of grief, eh?"

He scoffed. "A fat lot of comfort you'd be at any time. No, your purpose for being there is to entertain Cicely Talbot."

The name made me jump a bit. I'm pretty sure for a second or two I entirely left the chair and was airborne. "Not," I said, hopefully, "the same Cicely Talbot that was at Mother's Christmas party last year?"

"Of course that one! How many Cicely Talbots do you know?"

Here's the story. Christmas last year. Party. Everyone having a good time, mainly because I'd spiked the eggnog with a liberal amount of bourbon. The party consisted mostly of my mother's cronies, and I can't tell you how many forty- or fifty-year-old women pinched my ass that night or tried to trap me under the mistletoe. One even asked me to take her up to my bedroom to show her my "etchings." When I told her I had no etchings to show, she grinned lasciviously and said, "I don't give a shit, honey," and made a grab for my crotch. When I backed up to escape, I was unwittingly standing under the mistletoe and another middle-aged woman grabbed me and tried to shove her tongue down my throat.

The only person near my age at the party was a young writer, this Cicely Talbot. Small gal, with big brown eyes. To get away from the drunk and oversexed cougars, I sat on the couch to converse with Cicely.

The more we talked, the more she made cow eyes at me. And then she started to get a bit hands on. You know how it works. I'd say something funny and she'd laugh and put her hand up to her mouth as if she'd laughed too loud, and when the hand came back down, magically, it landed on my knee. Or my thigh.

Which struck me as odd, as I would have thought the conversation contained enough clues to enable anyone to figure out I was gay. I mean, if you pepper your speech with a lot of *my ex-boyfriend and I*s and *don't you think he looks hot?*s and *I can't stand Justin Bieber's music, but I'd do him in a hot New York minute*s, you'd think you wouldn't have to announce that you were gay. These tidbits weren't getting through, though. At one point, after downing another spiked nog, I was telling Cecily how action movies were better when the hero was shirtless when she suddenly turned to me and looked me straight in the eye.

"Let's get married," she said.

It was a good thing I'd already swallowed the nog, or I'd have done a spit take. As it was, I laughed uneasily. Surely she was joking.

She hadn't been.

I spent the rest of the party trying to stay away from her.

In the weeks after the Christmas party, it seemed wherever I went, there was Cicely Talbot. She was at every party I was. She shopped at the same supermarket. She was even in the men's underwear department at Macy's. It soon became apparent that I was being stalked. I had to change my phone number. It got to the point where I figured I'd have to resort to disguises when I went out, when the stalking abruptly ceased.

"She found some new guy to torture," a friend informed me. "She's smart as hell, but loony. She does this all the time, I hear. Fixates on some guy. Luckily for you, she's moved on."

I was happy for myself and said a prayer for the poor sod who replaced me.

Now it seemed I would be thrown back into her company. I made a face. "Why is she going to the reading of Charlotte Winston's will?" It really was beginning to sound like this was a new fad. *Hey, let's all go to hear the reading of Herbert Plonkslip's will!*

"Cicely has known the Winstons for years. The point is that she's going to be there, and I want you to try to act like a human being around her. Apparently she likes you, or so your mother tells me. Personally I can't think of a reason why anyone would do anything but loathe you. Why are you making that face?"

"It's just that… well, this Cicely squirt does seem to have taken a shine to me. Can't blame her, of course, but… well, she's barking up the wrong tree."

The stepmonster frowned. "What do you mean? Why can't you speak like normal people? What tree?"

I opened my mouth to expound but then thought of my mother and closed it. "Nothing," I muttered meekly.

Dollings frowned. "Cicely is writing a biography of Charlotte Winston, and for some unknown reason she's thinking of having it published by Miller and Sons. I want you to get her to publish the book with us."

I understood his desire to have the volume published by Dollings. It sounded unbearably dull, so it would fit right in with their normal stuff. Still, I was puzzled. "Why would anyone want to read about Caps… I mean, Jake's aunt? I'm sure she was a great old dame, full of life and kind to dogs and parakeets, but what makes her the subject of a book?"

The stepmonster rolled his eyes. "I wouldn't expect you to understand. You're too busy running around drinking, having parties, and playing video games. Charlotte Winston was a prominent woman in the area. She was involved in not only business, but politics. She was quite a woman."

I could hardly be blamed for not knowing these facts, as Caps hadn't included them in any conversations we'd had. Up until that morning, I'd not even known he'd had a Great-aunt Charlotte, let alone one who rubbed elbows with the chieftains of society. It hardly mattered. "I'll be glad to accompany you to the will shindig, mainly because Jake has already asked me, and I'll spare a moment to speak to Cicely about the wonders of publishing with Dollings Press, but don't expect me to do more than that. I'm not fond of the girl. At Mom's party she kept on wanting to discuss the poetry of Emily Dickinson with me. I'm not big on poetry and I certainly don't want to discuss the works of Mademoiselle Dickinson."

The glare the stepmonster gave me was dark and full of wrath. "You'll do more than that, you inexcusable sloth. Cicely, for some reason, is against publishing with us. She's unimpressed with our backlist, apparently. Told me so herself. Now, I've put up with you ever since I married your mother, and it's been a burdensome cross to bear. I finally have found something you can do for me, and, by thunder, you're going to do it! I want you to woo this young woman—"

"Woo?"

"Yes, woo! Don't they teach you basic English in that damned school of yours?"

"They do, but the last person who used the word 'woo' died around 1930, I believe."

"Whatever word you want to use, then! I want you to use your questionable charms to get this girl to see reason! For some reason, she thinks you're almost human. While we're there, I want you to flirt with her! Do whatever it takes! Then, when she's in the mood, I want you to get her to sign a contract with Dollings Press so that we get that book! Understand?"

I understood only too well. I could also hear the danger signals blaring in my ears. If, after just one long conversation with me at a Christmas party, the mad Cicely wanted to go ring shopping, what chance would I have if I put on the Weasley charm? Yes, she'd sign any contract put in front of her, but she'd also be picking out the names of our children and planning our golden wedding anniversary.

It seemed to me that I was to have an uncomfortable weekend, until I thought of a possible way out. "Surely, my dear stepdad, it wouldn't be the Christian thing to lead this woman on. I mean, it seems rather dastardly to flirt with a girl just to—"

I didn't get any further. The stepmonster placed his fist on the desk and raised himself out of his chair. "Don't you dare!" he thundered. "Don't you dare to try to tell me what's the Christian thing to do! For one thing, I think it would be a good idea for you to find a suitable girl to date. You spend way too much time with your friends. A man your age should be starting to look for his mate instead of playing *Donkey Kong* all night long."

I hadn't played *Donkey Kong* since I was in kindergarten, but it didn't seem like the time to point this out. "But I really don't like her!" I protested. "I'm pretty sure she's a lunatic. Asylums probably have her picture on the wall—*Have You Seen This Woman?*"

"You'll get to like her!" His face was crimson, and the veins in his neck were positively dancing. "You're going to do this, or I'll see that your allowance is cut off!"

I paled. No money for alcohol? No going out to the bars? The mind boggled. And I could see him getting Mom to agree to this only too well. A gem of a woman, but she was pretty pliant where the stepmonster was concerned.

The weekend wasn't looking very sunny.

Chapter Three

IT JUST goes to show that you can't always judge a book, as they say, by its cover. An odd phrase, because people do it all the time. I've done it myself. I recall browsing the mystery section of my local B&N and finding *Blood on the Doorstep*, which had an absolutely smashing cover with loads of dark colors brightened by drops of crimson. The cover simply screamed "There's lots of blood and mayhem inside here!" So much so that even though my wallet was on the thin side that week due to several parties and a pair of Nikes I had to have to replace the ones I destroyed escaping rabid and angry neighbors at one of those parties, I bought the book without even reading the blurb.

Well, imagine my disappointment when I got home and dove into the pages only to find that it lacked a corpse until nearly halfway through, and even then there was little bloodshed. The detective of the piece wandered around chatting with people and doing some cooking, probably wondering all the while, as I was, just where all the good murderers had gone for the summer.

My point is, if you looked at my life, you might think that Patrick Carrington Weasley had it pretty good. His mother, you'd point out, has to use a wheelbarrow to cart dough to the bank on Fridays. On top of that, she married the head honcho of Dollings

Press, a man who isn't hurting for cash himself. And the family home, a rambling Tudor-style structure set on a hill on the outskirts of Rockford, while an eyesore, couldn't be a bad place to be raised. Loads of room for hide-and-go-seek and other games for a child to enjoy.

This Patrick, or Weasel, you say, must have had a soft time of it, surrounded by all that money. And this is where I can tell you that you'd be wrong in saying such a thing.

True, when Dad was alive I usually had things pretty good. The latest video games. All the latest electronic gadgets. Loads of presents under the Christmas tree.

But somewhere along the road, something went wrong. It was decided by my mother, who read questionable books by people she'd seen interviewed on religious television programs, that my spiritual side was not being nourished. Thus at the age of ten I was sent packing to a boarding school run by Mrs. Climthorpe, a nut of the first order. Mrs. Climthorpe ruled with an iron hand and banned my reading of thrillers. The only book worth reading, in her opinion, was the Bible. While there are some pretty good murders in the Bible— Jael bashing Sisera's head in with a tent peg and a mallet springs to mind—there are relatively few detectives. Leaf through the thing. No Hercule Poirots, no Nero Wolfes, and not even a mention of Jessica Fletcher of *Murder She Wrote* fame. So I was a little pissed. Mrs. Climthorpe's was the first of many schools I was tossed out of.

After Dad died, things got worse. The stepmonster thought I should wear better clothes, so of course I began to favor T-shirts and jeans, rarely wearing anything else. He also cut my allowance down to a pittance, so at these schools I was attending I often had to beg off friends just to go to a movie or enjoy a burger on the weekend.

So, yes, in some ways I've had it good and in others I haven't. There are times when Mom's in a good mood and I can weasel (get it?) a little extra out of her, and I do have possession of a fabulous yellow Corvette, but things haven't always been rosy.

And the weekend at the Winston place looked to be one of the least rosy weekends ever.

I wasn't to head out to the late Charlotte Winston's domicile until Friday evening, so Thursday seemed like a good night to go out and party. True, I did have a few classes the next morning, but I'd already been to two of Professor Kinney's not-too-riveting Physics lectures that week, and one doesn't want to overdo that sort of thing. My Folklore class wasn't until eleven, and I figured I could rouse myself sufficiently to get to that. We'd been reading about tales of the vanishing hitchhiker—you know the tale, boy picks up girl along the road, drives her home, she vanishes, and he learns she's been dead lo these many years—and I wanted to stun the professor with my knowledge of Resurrection Mary, a famous Chicago-area spook who often thumbed a ride with the unwary. Therefore I pledged to be home and slumbered by three o'clock at the latest.

So as the clock struck eleven, Caps and I were having our driver's licenses examined with care by the 21 Club doorman. He handed mine back, his face full of suspicion. While I really had twenty-one candles on my last birthday cake, I couldn't blame him for his scrutiny. The Weasley genes had given me a boyish face, and the lack of a recent haircut had given me Little Lord Fauntleroy curls about the ears. He probably thought I was a high school kid who'd stolen his older brother's ID. He grunted. "You can go in," he said with the air of someone who's letting you get into the cookie jar when you really shouldn't.

The 21 Club had three bars within its walls. There was the big bar in the main room, with a large dance floor and a stage. The stage was bare on Thursdays, but on the weekends drag queens held court there over their subjects or occasionally the management would host a strip show. Downstairs were a smaller bar and several pool tables. Off to the side of the main bar was a smallish room with a smallish bar, which was where Caps and I headed. This bar was the only place in the 21 Club where you could converse without shouting, plus it had the added attraction of Dave the Barman. Dave wasn't young, nor was he particularly pretty, but he didn't skimp on the vodka when he was making drinks. On the rare night that Dave wasn't in attendance, we avoided the side bar like the plague, because they'd substitute Horrible Harry in Dave's place. Harry was not only the worst drinks mixer in the Midwest, but a notorious cockblocker.

A cockblocker, for those not in the know, is one who steals the boy you were planning on taking home right from under your nose. You'd spend an hour or two buying drinks for a young cutie only to go off to take a piss and come back and find Harry schmoozing the guy. "I get off at three," Harry would be saying, giving the boy his best come-fuck-me look. Enough to make a guy sick.

Luckily Dave was in position, so Caps and I settled on some stools while he prepared our Grey Goose and tonics. The main bar was beginning to fill up, and we could both hear and feel the thump of dance music from the sound system, but in the side bar things were on the quiet side. As quiet as things get in the 21 Club, anyway. At one end was a couple who looked like they were trying to devour each other's face and at the other was some poor guy who had already had a few too many. His head was down on the bar with his dark hair spilling over into a bowl of pretzels. The dude was out cold. I paid him and the ravenous couple little attention, wanting to get the lowdown from Caps.

"It's beginning to sound like quite the party," I said once Dave had delivered the drinks. "You, me, the stepmonster, Cicely Talbot, and goodness knows who else. Are there enough bedrooms, or are we expected to bunk together?"

Caps didn't look happy. "You don't know the half of it. There's Uncle Mark, who was Charlotte's husband. He's a good guy. I've always liked him. The house is big, so don't worry about room. Aunt Charlotte called the house Winston Manor."

"I like the sound of that. Sounds like a place in a murder mystery."

"And there will be lots of assorted relatives there. Aunt Ericka and her brat. I think my cousin Ned is coming. Keith Sutton, of course. And Tyler Kendrick."

I nearly choked on my Gray Goose. "Tyler Kendrick? What in the devil's name will he be doing there?"

"Didn't I tell you? Uncle Mark hired him as a part-time groundskeeper. Apparently Neanderthals have few talents, but they can manage to push a lawn mower and prune a rosebush."

"I thought that he'd joined the police force."

"Oh, he did. He just does the gardening stuff on the weekends."

Caps and I had known Kendrick since middle school, but while we had stayed thin and had pleasing temperaments, Tyler had grown into such a muscular hulk that professional wrestlers would look at him and cross to the other side of the street. While I enjoyed whacking a tennis ball or tossing bowling balls down alleys, Kendrick went into more violent sports. If he couldn't bloody an opponent's nose or chip a tooth, Tyler Kendrick wasn't interested. He was also a huge homophobe, one of those who believe every gay guy around lusts after his overdeveloped pectoral muscles. Last time I'd run into him, he'd been under the false assumption that I'd been "eying" him and had threatened to beat me to a pulp. Actually I'd been marveling at his poor taste in clothing.

I groaned and took a bigger than normal gulp of my drink. "This is going to be a nightmare," I stated, and then I filled Caps in on my stepmonster's plan for me to flirt with Cicely.

Caps laughed. "I wouldn't worry about that. She thinks you're so hot that all you'll have to do is bat your eyes and she'll sign on the dotted line."

"I hope you're right."

"What I can't understand is how she can't see that you're queer as fuck. The girl's gaydar must be broken."

"I wouldn't say I'm obviously gay."

"I would."

I was about to give Caps a pithy retort when the passed-out dude at the end of the bar snorted loudly. I glanced his way, thinking he was about to rouse himself, but he merely shifted his head, nearly upsetting the pretzel bowl. I looked more carefully at the guy. "There's something awfully familiar about him."

Caps followed my gaze. "I think that's McCaffrey."

"So it is. Is he ever conscious?"

"He was when he left my house. Woke up shortly after you left."

"Did he say anything?"

Caps thought a moment. "Not really."

"What's his first name? I'm assuming there's more than just McCaffrey."

"I'm sure there is, but damned if I know it. I've always heard him called McCaffrey."

As the young man showed no sign of coming out of his slumber, I returned my attention to Caps. "Anyway, about this will. Why is it taking a whole weekend to read it? Can't we just dash in, gather and read, and dash back out? Seems a pity to waste a good weekend on this gathering, especially as I'm not in the running to receive any bequests from this aunt of yours, as I never met her."

"The actual reading will be Sunday night, but Aunt Charlotte requested that everyone come for a weekend house party in her honor."

"She didn't request me."

"No, but I did. And so did your stepfather."

Dave asked us if we wanted another drink, which was a silly question. Armed with more alcohol, we decided to head into the main bar area to see if any hotties had arrived. I wouldn't say the place was jammed to the rafters like it was on the weekends, but it was fairly busy. I found me a cute Latino and asked him to dance. We hit the dance floor and bumped and ground against each other for a while. He ripped off his shirt midway through, revealing a taut, tight six-pack. We got hot and sweaty, so after a while we decided to take a break and hit the bar. While we waited for the bartender to fill our order, I took a look around. Caps was over near the door, talking animatedly with the twins, who had obviously just arrived. I'd known Donald and Darren for a little over a year now and I still couldn't tell them apart, although supposedly they weren't identical twins. Could have fooled me. Seeing that I and the Latino (he told me his name, but it's hard to hear with the music blasting in your ear) had vacated the dance floor, they waved us over. The Latino wanted to rejoin his own band of friends, so I walked over to Caps and the twins on my own.

"You've been missing all the fun," said Donald—or maybe it was Darren—with a laugh.

"What fun is that?"

Darren—or, at least, the one who hadn't spoken first—said, "Outside. There's a bunch of protesters from some church or other. We've been out there making fun of them."

I've never understood the reasoning behind the protesting some religious groups seem to enjoy. Do we go and picket monster truck rallies for their lack of glitter and glitz? Do gay throngs stand outside the Republican National Headquarters and demand they make "We Are Family" their theme song? "Sounds like fun. Are they still out there?"

Twin number one—we'll call him Donald just to keep things somewhat straight—chortled. "I'm sure they are. They're quite agitated now, especially after we mooned them."

"I'm sorry I missed that. Shall we go out and terrorize them some more? Let them know exactly how badly we've fallen into this life of sin?"

"Oh, let's!" the twins exclaimed in unison. The four of us linked arms and marched to the door, camping it up quite a bit and making sure we swished when we walked. The door to the 21 Club isn't broad enough to allow four gay guys through at once, even if all four are on the skinny side, so we formed a sort of chain. I emerged into the warm night air last.

Sure enough, across the street were about fifteen protesters, complete with signs saying things like "God Hates Fags" and "Repent" or "Go to Hell." One woman was attempting to stop people as they were heading inside the 21 Club to hand them pamphlets. She wasn't very successful.

I was laughing at the silliness of it all when I spotted a familiar face among the protesters. There, holding a "Fag Sin" sign and bellowing at the people heading into the club, was my stepmonster, Jasper K. Dollings.

Chapter Four

LUCKILY for me I'd come out the door last. The twins were in front of me, partially blocking me from view. I hunched down quickly, peeking around Donald's side to see if I'd been spotted. The stepmonster was too busy badgering some young couple strolling down the sidewalk to take any notice of me.

"Excuse me," I told the boys before, without straightening, I turned and waddled back inside the club. The doorman eyed me with even more suspicion as he noted my crablike gait.

"Crick in my back," I told him. "Too much dancing."

This didn't seem to satisfy him, but he said nothing. Working at a gay bar, he'd probably seen much stranger things than a guy entering nearly bent double. I walked a few more paces, making sure the door was firmly closed behind me, before unbending and putting myself in the full, upright position. Caps had followed me in, although the twins had stayed outside to enjoy the show the protesters were providing. Arching an eyebrow at me, Caps asked, "What's up with the walk? Are you attempting a Groucho Marx impression?"

"My stepmonster's out there!" I hissed.

"What? With the protesters?"

"No, he's out there with the twins, arranging a kinky three-way. Of course he's with the protesters! Fortunately, he didn't see me."

"He's bound to at some point, unless they give up and go home. I mean, you have to use the exit sooner or later. Unless the manager lets you go out the back way or something."

That sounded like a plan to me. The manager of the 21 Club and I weren't exactly best friends, as I'd been kicked out of the place three times in the short span of time since I'd turned twenty-one, but it was worth a shot. We found him sitting with some others at a small table near the stage. He was ogling the pretty boys dancing and didn't seem to want to take his attention away even as I put my case to him. When I finished he laughed.

"Sorry, kid. You'll just have to chance it that they disperse before you leave."

"Oh, come on," I said, giving him my best pleading look. "Surely there's a back or side entrance I can escape through."

"There is," he replied. He was keeping careful watch on my Latino. "It's alarmed, though."

"Surely you have a key, though. To shut off the alarm."

"Oh, I do." He paused to smile at his friends, who were also enjoying my plight. "I just can't remember where it is at the moment." They all laughed heartily.

Caps and I retreated to the side bar, where Dave, with only a glance at us, began to prepare fresh drinks without our even asking. He set them in front of me and Caps and asked, "Trouble?"

I told him. He nodded sympathetically. "Why don't you just get the manager to let you out the side door?"

"We asked him. He's being a dick."

Dave nodded again. "That sounds like him. Maybe the protesters will get tired and go home."

"They look like they're there for the long haul. I think they want to preach to the boys as they exit later on tonight." I emptied about half of my drink in one go. It didn't help.

"There is one other thing you could do," Dave said.

"HONEY, stop squirming," the young man with the blue eye shadow commanded. He pointed the tube of lipstick at me. "I may be a fairy, but this ain't no magic wand. Sit still and let Mama do her thing."

Even though there was no drag show that night, several of the girls/boys were gathered in the dressing room to work on their outfits for upcoming shows and generally bitch about other queens. Dave introduced me to Zach, also known as Kitty Mews. Zach seemed to always be at least part Kitty. He was wearing jeans so tight that I couldn't breathe and a shiny red shirt I'm pretty sure didn't come from the men's department of Macy's. There wasn't much to him—he couldn't have weighed more than 130 pounds soaking wet—but he frightened me a little. He had a flash in his eyes every now and then that said *Mess With Me And I'll Rip Your Eyeballs Out.* So I sat in his chair and let him transform me.

And transform me he did. I rented an outfit from him for a rather exorbitant price, and he provided me with a wig and painted my face. I wasn't allowed to look while he was working, but I could see Caps standing nearby, smirking. "Is it that bad?" I asked.

"On the contrary," Caps replied, nearly keeping a straight face. "I'd let any son of mine date you."

Zach gripped my chin and applied the lipstick. His grip was pretty fierce for such a little guy. "There," he said, capping the lipstick. "You can look now."

I swiveled in the chair to look in the mirror. My jaw dropped.

It wasn't me. I don't know who it was looking back at me, but it wasn't me. The wig was long and blonde, spilling about my shoulders. I was wearing a red gown with a split halfway up the side. Zach had wanted to shave my legs, but I was adamantly against that, so instead I wore pantyhose. I looked like a cross between Scarlet Johansson and Kristen Stewart, with a little Joan Rivers thrown in, as Zach had given me lips that wouldn't have looked out of place on Batman's enemy, the Joker.

"Holy shit," I said.

"You look like your mother, minus about twenty years," Caps chortled. "And don't sit like that. Cross your legs. I can see right up your skirt."

"Bite your tongue," I said, rearranging my legs in a more ladylike fashion.

Zach rummaged in one of his many bags, bringing out a pair of red high-heeled shoes. "You'll need these, honey. You can't wear that dress in flats. Heels make the rear end pop."

"I'm not sure I want my rear end to pop, and I don't think I can stand in those without toppling over."

Zach gave me a withering look. "Put them on. Don't make Mama smack you."

He was maybe a year older than me, so I don't know where the "Mama" came in, but I obeyed and slipped on the heels. I stood, feeling like a baby giraffe taking his first uncertain steps. "I must be six foot seven in these things!"

"You exaggerate your height as well, huh?" Caps said, laughing.

I tried to walk. I wobbled a bit, but stayed upright. "Aren't you going to get in the chair," I asked Caps, "and get your makeover?"

"My stepdad's not outside with a bunch of picketers. I can go out without a disguise, thank you very much!"

"But you can't go out with me! Dollings knows you!"

"I'll wait. We'll exit separately."

"I'll escort you out, honey," Zach/Kitty said. He took my arm. "You can lean on me if the heels get to be too much for you."

And so I left the 21 Club arm in arm with a short guy wearing eyeliner. By the time we hit the sidewalk, I had almost mastered the heels. Well, mastered them in the sense that I didn't wobble when I took a step. I was leaving my own clothes behind. I didn't care much about the T-shirt and jeans, but the Nikes were new. I'd have to shop in the morning before heading out to Winston Manor. Zach insisted I lean against him—not because he wanted to cuddle, but because he was afraid that I was going to snap off one of his heels. We must have looked like a loving couple when we strode across the street to the parking lot, approaching the protesters.

One woman, who I'm pretty sure was one of the Gorgons of ancient myth by the way her hair was arranged, snarled at us. "Faggots!"

Zach smiled sweetly at her. "You got that right, darling!"

My stepmonster glared at us. There was no hint of recognition in his eyes. "There's a special place in Hell reserved for people like you!"

"I hope," I said, speaking in a light, high tone unlike my usual voice, "it has a bar, because this queen is parched!" I looked down at Zach. "Come on, sweetie. Let's go back to your place for a nightcap."

There were more yells from the protesters, but we ignored them and headed to my car. I made sure my butt wiggled while I walked. Having been an actor in my past—in the third grade I was featured in the school play, winning the coveted part of Jumbo the Elephant—I knew how to live the part, as they say in theater parlance. The protesters quickly lost interest in us anyway, when other prey came out of the club. When we got to my car, I turned to give my benefactor a look of thanks. He, though, was staring at my Corvette.

"This is yours?" he asked in awe.

"Yep. She's a beauty, isn't she?"

Zach held out his hand. "I think I need another hundred."

"Dollars? I paid you for the dress rental, and if you're afraid you won't get it back—"

"For the makeover. That makeup don't come cheap, and it looks like you can afford it, chum."

"But... a hundred dollars!" I thought about arguing that my allowance wasn't quite the astronomical sum he seemed to think it was, but his resolute look told me I hadn't a chance. I opened the little clutch purse he'd provided and fished out my wallet. "You're an evil little queen, you know that, don't you?" I said as I forked over the money.

He smiled. "A girl's gotta do what a girl's gotta do." Shoving the Benjamin in his pocket, he said, "I'll wait until you pull out of the parking lot before heading back to the protesters. I want to offer to do the hair of that one woman who yelled at us. That girl needs help, in more ways than one."

I admit I may have spun my tires and made a bit of a racket pulling out of the parking lot. Once the gaggle of protesters was at a safe distance in my rearview mirror, I began to relax. I found it impossible to drive with those stupid heels on, so when I pulled up at the first stop sign I slipped them off. My estimation of those men and woman who endure that particular form of torture went up considerably.

I was getting close to home when my cell phone rang. It was Caps. I had a hard time getting to it because A: the phone was on the passenger seat in that stupid clutch purse and B: Zach had insisted on fitting me with some press-on fingernails and I had trouble flipping the phone open because I wasn't used to long pieces of plastic sticking out of the ends of my fingers. I eventually managed it.

"Getaway go okay?" Caps asked.

"Swimmingly. The stepmonster came right up but didn't recognize me. The little queen gouged me for an extra hundred before it was all over, but I guess it was worth it." I was approaching my street and was feeling pretty good, having gotten one past Daddy Dollings. "How are things at the club?" I could hear the thump-thump of the dance music in the background.

"Not bad. I've been dancing with your Latino."

"What's his name? I couldn't catch it."

"Heck if I know. He told me, but it seemed to have too many consonants and not enough vowels. That and I was drinking, so I wasn't really paying attention."

I had just pulled through an intersection and was turning onto my street when I was aware of a light show around me. Flashing lights and the whoop of a siren informed me that an officer of the law was requesting I pull over. I cursed aloud.

"What was that?" Caps asked.

"I'm being pulled over. I'll have to call you back," I said.

My feeling of bonhomie changed to one of sinking dread. I stopped the car along the curb and sat there waiting while the cop ran my plates. It occurred to me that I was in for some ribbing for my attire. I was also wondering why he'd stopped me. True, I'd been going a few miles over the speed limit—Corvettes like to stretch their legs and it's hard to get them to behave—but I wasn't going too fast at the time his lights had danced about the night sky. And while one isn't supposed to talk on cell phones while driving, I wasn't aware that they were pulling you over for that infraction. My seat belt was on. Maybe I had a taillight out?

After what seemed an eternity, the officer got out of the squad car and came up to my window. I thought a little charm wouldn't hurt, so, license and registration in hand, I turned and flashed him a smile.

It was Tyler Kendrick.

Chapter Five

I'M SURE that I paled under the rouge Zach had applied. I tried to say something, but all that came out of my mouth was some sort of a weak groan. My hand ceased to maintain the ability to grip and the documents in my hand fell into my lap.

"Evening, miss," Kendrick said, tipping his hat slightly.

Words still weren't coming to me. My mouth moved around a bit, but I could only emit inarticulate sounds. I may have whimpered some. I knew that somehow Kendrick was going to find some way of hauling me downtown and I was going to be in a cell overnight with guys named Clyde and Buddy while I was dressed like a hooker.

Strangely, there seemed to be a smile on Kendrick's face. Not an *Aha! I got you* smile, but a smile like the ape was thinking pleasant thoughts.

"Is this your vehicle, miss?" he asked. Although he was standing still, there was a swagger in the way he spoke. They must teach swagger at cop school.

It was on my tongue to say, "Of course this is my vehicle, you lumping ignoramus," but I stopped myself. He'd used the term "miss" as his form of address. Could it be that the big lummox really thought I was a female? And the smile he bore was one I'd seen before, at the bar when someone was trying to pick me up. I blinked. If I revealed at this point that I was his hated acquaintance Patrick Weasley, aka Weasel, he'd go ballistic. Homophobes hate to admit, even to themselves, that they find another guy attractive, even if said guy is dressed as a frankly attractive woman and is being viewed in a darkened car on a dimly lit street. I cleared my throat and tried to sound like Megan Fox. "No, officer, this car belongs to my cousin. He let me borrow it." God help me, I actually thrust out my chest, giving Kendrick a good look at the breasts Zach had concocted for me. The bra was filled with foam.

The smile broadened. "And your cousin's name?"

"Patrick Weasley."

Kendrick nodded. "I think I know him. We went to school together. You're his cousin, you say?"

"That's right, officer."

He nodded at the documents on my lap. "I'll need to see the registration and your license, miss."

License. Oh, shit. Kendrick wasn't the brightest thing on God's green Earth, but even he would be able to see that the license was for a six-foot-one male with blond hair and piercing blue eyes, weighing 155 pounds. I fumbled with the papers, managing to hand him the registration. "I've got this. I was looking through my purse, but I seem to have mislaid my license. I was attending a charity ball tonight, in aid of orphaned children, and I'm afraid I was running late and grabbed the wrong purse."

I felt like my heart was going to explode. I watched his face as the smile disappeared and was replaced by a frown. "You really should have your driving license on you when operating a motor vehicle, miss," he said sternly.

When operating a motor vehicle? I thought cops only talked like that on television. I was desperate. I looked up at him pleadingly. "It won't happen again, officer."

He made a cursory examination of the registration and handed the slip back to me. "Well, I only pulled you over because you rolled through that stop sign back there, plus you were talking on your cell phone. You need to make sure that you come to a full stop before going through an intersection like that."

"Oh, of course, officer! I'm so sorry. It won't happen again." I was so scared I was afraid I was going to pee my pants, or more exactly, Zach's gown.

The smile came back to Kendrick's face and he leaned against the door, putting his face close to mine. "I should issue you a warning ticket, but I'll let it pass this time." He pulled out a spiral notebook and a pen. "I will need your name, address, and phone number, though, since you don't have your license on you."

The nerve of the man! He was using his uniform and the office accorded to him to pick up girls! In this case, girls who weren't even girls! He should be reported to his superiors! However, I realized I was hardly in the position to lodge a complaint, so I tried to act demure. "My name is Kitty," I said. Then I stopped. I couldn't use Mews as a last name. What the hell was my last name going to be? I glanced around. I looked at the steering wheel. No, Kitty Wheel was a stupid name. "Kitty Wells. The Kitty is short for Katharine."

Kendrick wrote. "That's a very pretty name."

I giggled. It sounded fake to me, but he seemed to fall for it. "Thank you." I gave him my actual street but changed the number. He wrote more, then asked me for my phone number. I rattled it off. It didn't occur to me until the last number had left my mouth that I'd given him my real cell phone number. I nearly punched myself in the face. It only showed how nervous I was, but it's ingrained in a person when someone asks for your number to just say it.

Kendrick put away the notebook and pen with a grin. "Strange," he said, "you being related to Weasel. I mean Patrick. We always called him Weasel."

"He's had that nickname for ages. Although I don't know why you think it strange that we're related."

He leaned in further. "It's just that—well, let's just say that you got all the looks in the family. I don't suppose you're single, by any chance?"

I thought about putting my high heels back on, stepping out of the car, and kicking him in the balls, but that might get me into trouble. I thought about telling him I was married to a police captain, but then my evil side came up with an even nastier notion. I pictured dear old Tyler Kendrick going home and jerking off, thinking of me in drag as he spewed his juice. I tossed my hair—well, the wig hair—back and laughed. "I'm not seeing anyone currently, if that's what you mean."

"Maybe I could call you sometime."

"Maybe you could." I batted my eyes.

We said our good-byes and he returned to his squad car. It may have been my imagination, but he seemed to be walking a little stiffly.

I DIDN'T give much thought to Kendrick after speeding away. However, I did ponder over him as I packed for the weekend. I remembered he'd be at Caps's great-aunt's place, doing his weekend gardening, but I figured he'd be outdoors most of the time, pruning rose bushes or planting begonias. With luck, I wouldn't even run into him. And if I did, I just had to remember that I had a cousin named Kitty Wells, should he inquire about her.

The next day I returned wig, gown, and shoes to Zach and then met up with Caps to drive out to the country for a weekend of listening to a will being read and rubbing elbows with publishing people. We took his car because if you put two people and baggage into a Corvette there isn't enough room left for air. It was late Friday afternoon when we left the city behind. As we zipped along past cow fields and corn, I tried to find something positive to think of, as the next several days promised, it seemed to me, to be a snorefest.

"Alcohol," I said.

"Pardon?" Caps asked.

"I'm hoping there will be loads of alcohol at your aunt's place."

"I'm sure there will be. Uncle Mark never let the bar get too depleted. Plus you know what those publishing types are like. They aren't much good unless they have a martini in their hands."

I nodded. The weekend was looking up. All I had to do was schmooze a writer for my stepfather, fix Caps up with the love of his life, and endure a few boring lunches and dinners. I'd packed my Kindle, loaded with my Conan Doyles, a few Agatha Christies, and a new one called *Murder in Poughkeepsie* by Diane Venz, an author I hadn't tried before. If nothing else, I could barricade myself in my room and read mysteries until it was time to depart.

We'd driven along for quite a while before Caps did a lot of turns onto country roads and finally announced, "There's the house. Up there on the left."

It was a monstrosity. At one point it had been painted a dark blue, but time and the elements had reduced it to a dingy gray. The house was Victorian in design, with lots of gingerbread trim and even a tower room looming on one side. Charles Addams would have looked at the place and said, "You've gone too far with the Gothic look, folks." Poe would have shaken his head sadly and muttered that even he would give the place a wide berth. To say it was gloomy would be to understate its utter bleakness. I turned to glare at Caps.

"You say the place only has two ghosts? I'd say that ghosts were missing a good opportunity here. You late aunt's house seems like it'd be a haven for the dearly departed."

"It's not as bad as that," Caps protested.

"It's not? At the end of the weekend, do we get to pull the mask off the Phantom Mariner so that he can say that he would have gotten away with it if it hadn't been for us meddling kids?"

Caps frowned. "We don't have a Phantom Mariner. Not that I've heard of, anyway."

There was a big garage to the rear of the house where a cluster of cars was already parked. The garage was obviously a more recent addition to the property and looked infinitely more cozy and welcoming than the house. We added Caps's car to the bevy of vehicles and got out. I looked around. Other than the spooky house, the property itself didn't look bad: A vast lawn, dotted with the occasional tree. An aged barn that had seen better days, but one I'd stay in as opposed to the house any day. There was even a little stream that could be seen at the back part of the property. Off in the distance I could hear cows. At least, I hope they were cows. Could have been dyspeptic pigs, for all I knew.

A fiftyish-looking man was approaching us from the direction of the house. He seemed a jolly sort, a broad smile on his face and a welcoming attitude. He embraced Caps warmly.

"Jake, my boy!" he said. "Glad you could come. We'll need a bit of life around the place this weekend."

They released each other and Caps introduced him as his Uncle Mark. Winston beamed at me. "Any friend of Jake's is more than welcome. Sorry you couldn't be here at a more pleasant time."

"This is Weasel, Uncle," Caps said. "I've told you about him."

Mark Winston looked at me again, this time with a little pity in his eyes. "Ah, then you're the stepson of old Jasper Dollings. Sorry about that."

"So am I."

"Can't be pleasant, seeing that sour old face whenever you go to see your mother."

"It isn't." I found myself really liking Caps's uncle. He not only was a good judge of character, but he also had a way with words.

"He hasn't arrived yet. Maybe we'll be lucky and he'll have had something come up at the last minute and he'll have to cancel. Can't think why Charlotte wanted to have a weekend party for her wake in the first place. Silly idea. Not like she can enjoy it, huh?" He slapped me on the arm.

His words made it sound like he was taking his wife's passing lightly, but there was sadness in his eyes. He was trying to play the genial host and, it seemed to me, had chosen to hide his grief in order not to bring everyone's mood down. I smiled at him. "It does seem like something out of an old mystery movie, having everyone gather for the reading of the will."

His face darkened at the mention of the will. "Yes, the will. Need to talk to you boys about that. Something has come up, and I—" He broke off when he realized someone else had come out of the house and was heading our way. "Tell you later," he said to Caps as the newcomer came closer.

My heart sank as I saw Cicely Talbot approaching. She seemed even smaller and mousier than I remembered. She was dressed in a dark pants suit and had on sunglasses even though the sun was giving it up for the day and was rapidly disappearing over the horizon. Although I couldn't see her eyes, I knew they were fixed on me. "I was wondering when the two of you would show up," she said brightly.

"Just got here," I said for lack of anything better to say.

Cicely barely acknowledged Caps and his uncle. She clamped onto my arm like a barnacle and smiled up at me. "I haven't seen you in simply ages!" she said with a hint of displeasure. "If I didn't know better, I'd say you were avoiding me. I would have thought you'd have called me."

I rarely call the boys I sleep with, let alone slightly older girls who can't tell a homo when they see one. I nearly jumped back, ready to make the sign of the cross with my fingers to ward her off before I remembered the mission Dollings had assigned me. I managed a weak grin. "Oh, you know. School and all that stuff."

"Well, we've got all weekend to get reacquainted," she gushed. "Has Jacob told you that I'm writing a biography of his aunt? Mr. Winston here has been kind and is letting me stay at the house here while I'm finishing it up. Luckily for you, I'm ahead of schedule, so I won't have to take time out to write and can spend all my time with you."

"Great," I said. I tried but failed to put any enthusiasm in the word.

She didn't notice. Still with a vise clamp on my arm, she began to lead us to the front door. "It's sad that Charlotte died before she could see the completed book, but it will be a fine memorial for a great woman."

I was sure the six people who would read the book would be thrilled, but I refrained from giving that opinion voice. Instead I said, "I'll have to get a copy when it comes out." I had no intention of doing so, but it sounded good.

"I'll make sure you get a signed copy," Cicely said with a squeak.

We had started to head to the house, but the sound of a car approaching made us all pause to see who was arriving. I figured, with my luck, that it would be the stepmonster. The car wasn't one of his, though. It was a huge black Cadillac. Mark Winston groaned when he saw it.

"Just what I needed," he muttered as he shook his head.

The vehicle rocked to a halt not far from where we stood. I could see three occupants inside. The driver and the other passenger got out. They were both fairly big guys, the type who go to the gym more often than they shower and who like to work out in front of mirrors so they can watch their muscles getting bigger. The driver opened the rear door to let out the third man, an older guy who, while not as Schwarzenegger as the other two, was no toothpick himself. This large specimen had a cigarette dangling out of his mouth. He took a puff and blew out the smoke as the two muscle dudes stood behind him, arms crossed and legs spread. They looked like Michael Jackson's bodyguards who had only just realized their charge was dead and were a little pissed off about it. The older dude tossed his cigarette onto the ground and stomped on it, looking around with a sneer.

"Nice day, Winston," he said. He had one of those voices that sounded like he gargled with gravel.

"What are you doing here, Smothers?" Winston didn't attempt to hide his displeasure.

A smile stole across the man's features. It wasn't a happy smile. More like the smile of a python that's just spotted lunch. "Just a neighborly visit, I assure you. I wanted to convey my condolences over Charlotte's death. She was quite a lady."

"Well, thank you. Now, if that's all—"

The older man, whose name was Smothers if I'd heard Caps's uncle correctly, shrugged his big shoulders. "I wanted to have a little chat with you. There are some rumors going around that have me worried."

I looked at Winston and then back at the man with the two bruisers standing behind him. It was an odd scene. I felt like I'd been dropped into one of those gangster flicks but, having missed the first bit, was unsure of the plot. Winston hadn't moved and the three muscle guys remained by the car, so voices had to be raised in order for the conversation to flow. I didn't blame Winston for not approaching this Smothers guy, though. The air around him and the two Incredible Hulks behind him fairly dripped with menace.

"What rumors? And why would they be of any concern to you, Smothers?"

Smothers's smile broadened. "I might be of some help to you. Word has it that not much of Charlotte's money is going to you, and you'll find it hard to keep up this big house without her considerable fortune."

Winston looked disgusted. "Oh, and I suppose you want to help out by offering to buy my Zopfi! Well, you can forget it, Smothers. You and your sons can get back in your car and go on home. The Zopfi isn't for sale, and besides, the rumors are unfounded. Despite what you may have heard—and I don't know where you could have heard such drivel—I have it on good authority that I'm Charlotte's main beneficiary. So I don't need any help from you, thank you very much."

The smile barely wavered. "I mean to have that Zopfi, Winston!"

I didn't know what a Zopfi was, but it must have been something pretty fantastic to cause all the testosterone to fly. Winston and the Smothers dude were facing each other like gunfighters at the OK Corral.

"*Man With Gazelle* belongs in my collection," Smothers said with finality.

"Then you should have bid higher on it at the auction," Winston replied.

I was even more confused with the introduction of this guy with a gazelle. Maybe this Zopfi guy had odd pets. Smothers's next statement cleared everything up.

"I want that painting, Winston."

Ah. So *Man With Gazelle* was a painting, presumably by this Zopfi guy. Caps's uncle owned the painting and this Smothers dude wanted it and was trying to look intimidating with his goon sons flanking him. All was clear. The intimidation was working on me, but not so much Winston, who was pale but determined in his manner.

"Like I said, Smothers, it isn't for sale."

Smothers took out a pack of cigarettes and stuck one into his mouth. Goon A didn't move a muscle, but Goon B quickly pulled out a lighter and lit the cigarette. His task accomplished, he resumed his position behind his father.

"We'll see, Winston. We'll see." Smothers let out a big puff of smoke. It drifted back and hit Goon A in the face. Goon A stifled a cough. It's hard to look menacing if you're coughing your lungs up. The elder Smothers suddenly turned and Goon B held the door open for him. "You haven't heard the last of this, Winston. I mean to have that painting."

We watched as the goon party got back into the Caddy and drove off. Once there was some distance between him and the car, Mark Winston led out a relieved sigh. "I hate that man," he said.

"He didn't seem very nice," Cecily said.

Caps looked worried. "What was that all about, Uncle?"

"I'll tell you later."

His head hung with obvious worry, Winston led the way as we headed to the house. Cecily chattered inanely, holding onto his elbow, in an attempt to cheer him up. Caps and I brought up the rear. I looked at my friend. "Do you have any idea what's going on?"

Caps shrugged. "I'm not sure. The Smothers live about a mile or so down the road. The father, Dominic Smothers, has quite an extensive art collection. Apparently Uncle Mark has a painting he wants."

"And the two goons?"

Caps smiled. "The goons are the Smothers brothers, Howard and Brandon."

"The Smothers brothers? You're joking, right?"

"That's what everyone calls them."

They looked more like MMA fighters than folksinging comedians, but I let the matter lie as we had arrived at the front porch. Winston ushered us inside. The interior of the house wasn't as bad as I'd thought it would be. True, it was dark and full of mahogany tables and vases and grandfather clocks and bric-a-brac, but there were no cobwebs and Dracula wasn't lurking in the shadows bellowing, "Velcome!" We paused in the foyer to take off our jackets—me, my hoodie—and I found myself looking up at the ceiling to make sure there wasn't a chandelier ready to fall and crush my skull. There wasn't, but I felt one couldn't be too careful. It looked like the type of house simply loaded with chandeliers poised to fall onto skulls.

"Isn't this place wonderful!" Cecily said, totally misinterpreting my gaze. "Staying here has been like a dream come true for me."

I had a dream like that when I'd eaten a whole Domino's pizza right before bedtime.

"Right now we're short on staff," Winston said apologetically. "We've only got a part-time housekeeper, but Mrs. Donleavey handles the meals and I've hired a young man from town to help serve."

I think he was worried about us looking down our noses because we had to hang up our own jackets and deposit them in the hall closet. He needn't have worried. I've been hanging up my own hoodies since I was twelve.

"The place hasn't changed much since I was here last," Caps observed.

His uncle smiled wanly. "Let me show you the library so you can see my latest acquisition. Zopfi's *Man With Gazelle* is worth every penny I paid for it!"

A short trip down a gloomy hall brought us to the aforementioned library. I would have liked to peruse the volumes to see if he had any Rex Stouts or Agatha Christies, but Winston led us directly over to the fireplace. To one side was a portrait of a woman. Caps told me that this was his late Great-aunt Charlotte. Above the mantelpiece was another painting, which Winston pointed out, his face beaming.

"My Zopfi!" he said.

I tried to look appreciative, but it wasn't easy. I figured it must have set back Caps's uncle a pretty penny, since other collectors seemed to be jealous of his owning it and other collectors generally don't concern themselves unless the said item is of value, but it was hard to imagine there was much value to this Zopfi thing. There was a biggish sort of blob I assumed was the man of the title, but only the number of legs led me to this conclusion. The other blob may have been a gazelle but it could easily have been a dog, a fire hydrant, or St. Paul's Cathedral, for all I knew.

Cecily, coming up beside me, sighed dreamily. "Isn't it something?"

"It's definitely something," I agreed.

"The use of color. The mood it sets. It's simply stunning."

That was true. I definitely felt stunned. As for mood, well, if this Zopfi guy was going for a gloomy, depressing, I-paid-how-much-for-this-piece-of-crap mood, then he'd hit the nail on the head.

Winston, though, was gazing at it lovingly. It takes all sorts, I suppose. "Charlotte and I had very different tastes in art. You wouldn't believe how much she paid that charlatan Maddox to paint her portrait." He waved a hand toward the portrait off to the side, dismissing the work. "In comparison, the Zopfi was a steal."

My tastes ran more to the portrait, in which, although the subject was a bit haughty looking and didn't seem like someone you'd want to spend an evening with, she at least resembled something that resided in the same universe as us. I wasn't as sure about the Zopfi.

Cecily sighed again and clutched my elbow, leaning her head against my shoulders. A chill ran through me. It had been a while since the days I was stalked by Cecily, and I had assumed she had given up and gone after other fish, ones that were more willing to bite. Her manner now was, if anything, even more familiar than ever, as if the months of not seeing Weasel had only made her heart, as they say, grow fonder. My knees felt weak.

"Any chance," I asked my host, "that I could see my room now?"

I HOLED up in my room until dinner was announced, mainly because I wanted to avoid running into Cecily as well as the stepmonster, whom we heard arriving as we exited the library. Winston told us that because of late arrivals, food would be served at nine o'clock in the dining room. With a half hour to spare, I stretched out on my bed and powered up my Kindle to begin Doyle's *The Man With the Twisted Lip*. Doctor Watson was just getting acquainted with the denizens of an opium den when there was a knock at my door.

"Yes?" I asked rather nervously. I had horrible visions of Cecily coming to my room and trying to ravage me.

"It's me," Caps replied, poking his head around the door. "Can I come in?"

I bade him enter. Caps slunk in. He was wearing different clothes and was a little dressier than his normal self. A sudden pang hit my brain. I hadn't thought about it, but what if they dressed for dinner? That was the one good thing that came from being shipped off to schools for most of my life. I missed all that being at homes where the rich hobnobbed, dressing for dinner and sipping sherry in the drawing room. I hated dressing up. All I'd brought was mostly jeans and some T-shirts. No one warned me that I'd have to be presentable. Caps saw my worried brow and gave me a reassuring wave. "Don't worry. Guests can show up to meals stark naked if they wish. Being one of the family, though, I've got to put on a show. What do you think?"

"You've even combed your hair. I don't think I've ever seen your hair combed."

"That's for Keith. I want him to see what a lovely shade of brown my eyes are."

"Are your eyes brown?"

"Yeah. What color would you say they were?"

"Sort of a muddy green."

Caps frowned. "You're going to have to do better than that. You can't get Keith to fall for me by saying things like, 'Doesn't he have the softest muddy green eyes you've ever seen?'"

"I have no intention of saying anything whatsoever about your eyes. Don't worry. I'm a pretty good matchmaker. This Keith guy will be humping your leg like a lovelorn spaniel by Sunday night."

"I'm counting on you, Weasel."

"You keep on stressing that like you're worried I'll let you down."

"That's what I'm afraid of." He wandered around the room listlessly, tapping nervously on top of the dresser and opening up the closet for a peek. "I see you've unpacked already."

"I've been hiding out in here, avoiding contact with the human leech."

"Cecily? She's not so bad."

"You haven't had her fingernails dug into your forearm."

Caps grinned, a little evilly, it seemed to me. "She does have a thing for you."

"Plus, I thought I heard someone trimming hedges out there earlier. Surely Kendrick isn't here already? It's Friday night. Shouldn't he still be in town, stopping helpless girls to get their phone numbers?"

"I believe Kendrick got here shortly after we did. And you probably did hear him out in the garden. He loves it out there. Says that it soothes his nerves after spending his days chasing criminals."

I scoffed and told Caps about what had happened after I left the club. He laughed heartily when I'd finished.

"That's rich!" he said between chortles. "If you like, I can see if there's still one of my aunt's old wigs around here and you can reacquaint him with… what did you tell him your name was?"

"Kitty Wells. She's supposed to be my cousin."

"Poor gal," Caps replied, running a hand over the hangers in the closet as if he were playing the xylophone. "Didn't you bring anything other than T-shirts?"

"There's one button-down shirt in there."

"It's a bowling shirt."

"It still buttons down."

"Why did you bother hanging them up? It's not like you've got anything in here that looks nice."

"I didn't. My bags were all unpacked and things hung up when I got in here."

"Ah, that'll be Turner. He's the guy that Uncle Mark hired to help out over the weekend. Aunt Charlotte used to get someone in from town whenever they'd have one of these big parties. Uncle Mark went one step further and hired a sort of butler for a few days."

"I bet he's a scary old codger that sneaks up behind you when you least expect it and says 'Dinner is served' in your ear, making you jump three feet in the air."

A knock at the door just then made Caps and me both start. I swung my legs off the bed and, after a throwing Caps a questioning frown, went to answer it.

I found Mark Winston lurking out in the hall. He came in, ensuring the door was securely closed behind him. "I wanted to catch you two boys before dinner. I've got something important to discuss with Jake, but I think maybe I should include both of you in the discussion. You look like a resourceful young man, Patrick, and Jake may need some help with this. I know you don't know me from Adam, Patrick—"

"Call me Weasel. Everyone does."

"I prefer Patrick. Anyway, Jake will tell you that I'm normally one of the most honest and aboveboard people you can meet."

"You're one of the best, Uncle," Caps said.

"So the favor I'm going to ask you may come as a surprise. I want you to steal your Aunt Charlotte's will."

Chapter Six

THERE was quite a silence after this statement. Caps, still standing by the closet, gripped hold of the doorframe as if he needed holding up. "Why on earth," he asked, incredulous, "would you need us to steal the will?"

"Well, not steal. Replace would be a better word. I want you and your friend here to take this older will," Mark said, holding up a thick envelope, "and put it in the place of the new will."

"The question still stands," Caps said. "Why? What's going on?"

The older man sighed heavily. "May I sit?"

"Certainly," I said.

Mark Winston sank gratefully into an armchair over by the window. He rubbed his temple as if to rid himself of a particularly nasty headache. "Your aunt, I'm afraid to say, Jake, went through a sort of phase in the last few months of her life."

"In what way?" Caps asked.

"She had an affair. With the gardener."

Both Caps and I stared. I sat back down on the edge of the bed, uncertain that my legs would keep me up. "With Kendrick?" I asked.

Winston nodded. "That's the fellow."

"But," Caps said, "she was thirty years older than him!"

"I think," Winston said bitterly, "that that was part of the attraction."

"But… Kendrick?" I asked.

"And she left him a bundle in her will. Had a new one drawn up. That's why I want you to replace the new one with the old. I'll be hanged before I allow that bastard to get a cent of her money. I've only kept him on because he suspects that she left him something, and I want to see his face when he's left out entirely."

I could see where the guy was coming from. It was kind of a slap in the kisser, your wife leaving lots of dough to her young lover, who was working right under your nose. Still, the whole replacing wills scenario seemed iffy.

"Did she know that you knew?" Caps asked, still looking like he might keel over. "That she was having an affair with Kendrick, I mean."

"Good Lord, no. She thought she was sly and discreet about it. She used to stand over at the window, though, and drool when he'd take his shirt off to mow the lawns. That was what first tipped me off."

I thought we needed to get past the affair angle, mainly because it turned my stomach. I raised a valid point. "Isn't what you're suggesting somewhat illegal? And how would we get away with it anyway? Surely loads of people know that she made out a new will. Lawyers, witnesses, that sort of thing. Won't they know there's been a switcheroo?"

Winston shook his head. "The new will is from one of those store-bought will kits. I'm not even sure they're legal in the state of Illinois—"

"They probably are," I interjected, not wishing to rain on his parade but wanting to view things sensibly.

"She had the cook and the cleaning woman witness this new will. They never read it. They'll have no idea. As far as her lawyer goes—he's downstairs now, by the way—the only will he's aware of is the one he drew up for her years ago, when she wasn't being unduly influenced by a young whippersnapper with overdeveloped muscles. Morally, I feel I'm in the right. The lawyer knows her current will, the one he's supposed to read tomorrow night, is in the safe in the library. I just want you boys to replace the old with the new, or rather, the new with the old."

Caps frowned. "There's a safe in the library? I've never noticed it."

"It's behind Charlotte's portrait. Set into the wall."

It figured. This old house seemed like the kind of place that would have a safe behind a portrait.

"Why don't you do it, Uncle?" Caps asked. "Seems like it should be an easy task. Just open the safe and—"

"I don't know the combination," the uncle replied miserably.

That seemed to me a problem. "How," I asked, "are we supposed to open it, then?"

Winston looked at me as if he'd forgotten I was there. "That's easy," he said. "Freeman—that's the lawyer—keeps the combination in his notebook, which is in his briefcase, which is in his room. All you have to do is excuse yourself during dinner, hop up to his room, and get the combination. Then tonight, after everyone's asleep, you switch the wills. No one will be the wiser."

I looked over at Caps, who seemed a bit green about the gills. "I hope you have fun with this, because you're on your own if you agree to it. I'm out."

Caps stared at me. "You won't help out?"

"Can't see why I would. Like I said, I'm sure we'd be breaking several laws, and with a cop on the premises—and one that hates my guts on top of that—there's no way I'll participate. But have fun. I'll just enjoy my dinner and retire early and find out what is going on with Holmes, Watson, and the dude with the unfortunate lip."

Caps shook his head sadly. "Some friend you are."

"A friend that wants to stay out of jail. Besides, other than sticking it to Kendrick, which I admit is a good reason, what's all this got to do with me?"

"Nothing," Winston said. "I was only including you if you wanted to join in. Jake, however—"

"Can't do it."

Winston frowned. "What do you mean, can't do it?"

"You know how nervous I get. I can't even watch action movies without taking a Dramamine. There's no way I could pull something like that off."

Winston shrugged. "Fine. There's a Porsche out in the garage that I was going to give you as a reward for doing this little deed, but—"

"I'll do it," Caps said with certainty.

THE certainty wavered after the uncle, leaving the old will in our care, left the room to see how dinner was progressing. "I can't do it, Weasel. No way. You're going to have to help me."

My laugh was hollow. "I wouldn't do it for all the Porsches in Rockford. Why should I? I'm not in either will. I don't have any vested interest, so to speak."

"I'll tell Kendrick that you're Kitty Wells," Caps said, his face set in stone.

I smiled weakly. "Don't kid about such things. He'd beat the crap out of me. And that would be just for starters."

"I'm serious, Weasel. I'll tell him unless you help out."

"You wouldn't," I protested, although the look in his eyes told me otherwise.

"I'm desperate, Weasel. You've got to help me. Just get the combination from the lawyer's room during dinner for me. I'll do the actual switching. Come on, Weasel. You've done more illegal things than this without batting an eye."

"I'm pretty sure running a stop sign doesn't top tampering with legal documents," I said with a grumble. I sighed. I wanted to help out Caps in any way possible, especially as the John Adair incident was still rankling deep within his bosom. He gave me his best puppy dog eyes. I caved. "All right, I'll do it. But I'll just get the combination. After that, you're on your own."

Caps came over to the bed and patted me on the shoulder. "You're one of the best, Weasel."

I COULDN'T get back into the Doyle story after Caps departed. There was too much on my mind. I had a lot I was supposed to accomplish in the next day or so. One: unite Caps and Keith Sutton. Two: Convince Cecily that she should publish her horrid little biography with my stepmonster's firm. Three: Rifle through a lawyer's room to steal the combination for a safe. And four: Keep as much as possible out of Kendrick's way. I didn't want him suddenly realizing that Cousin Kitty's voice was amazingly like mine, just raised an octave or two. Even Holmes would have found my conundrum difficult, calling it a four-pipe problem before locking himself in his room, hoping the whole thing would just blow over given enough time.

I didn't smoke pipes, so I paced the room until it was time for dinner.

While no one actually wore a tux for dinner, I did notice that I was the only person wearing a T-shirt and jeans. Most of the men wore sports jackets and ties, and the women were nicely decked out in dresses or at least tasteful outfits. The stepmonster, sitting on the other side of the table, eyed me like I was something he'd stepped on and needed to scrape off his shoe. I wished I hadn't wasted time pacing my room and had borrowed something from Caps to wear, but at the time pacing had seemed like the thing to do.

I was seated with Cecily Talbot on one side and one of Charlotte's sisters on the other, this one being Caps's Aunt Ericka. There were about fifteen or so people at the table, and I gave up trying to remember who was who. I did take note of the sole youngster in the group, who sat next to Aunt Ericka. I learned this young tyke, aged about twelve if my age-guessing skills were any good, was named Ernie and was the son of Ericka Winston. Before dinner commenced, Ericka coldly told the kid that the little cage he had on the table would have to be placed under his seat.

"I won't have that thing on the table," she told him.

Reluctantly, the kid complied. Curious, I tried to see what was in the cage as he stowed it away. The kid smiled at me.

"It's my spider, Jeffrey. He's a tarantula."

"Yes, he certainly seems to be."

"He's my pet."

"Better you than me. I'm not overly fond of spiders. Too many legs."

"No," Ernie said simply, "he's got the right number."

I took stock of the others around whom I needed to memorize. I easily spotted the nurse, Keith Sutton, but he was seated too far away from me to engage in conversation. I could see why Caps had fallen for the guy, though. He was a looker. Nice, rugged physique. Sweet smile. He reminded me a bit of Marky Mark as he was transitioning himself back to being Mark Wahlberg.

Sutton was chatting amiably with the other person I needed to keep filed away in my head, and that was the lawyer, Freeman. I learned when introductions were being passed around that his first name was Ebert. He was a cold old coot. When I remarked that I'd never heard of anyone with the first name Ebert and asked if people called him Eb, he fixed a stony glare on me and said that no, it was Ebert and that no one called him Eb. Although the lawyer was involved in the conversation with the nurse, he didn't seem to be enjoying it. I wondered if he ever enjoyed anything. Maybe death and will reading. He looked like he was itching to open the safe and do a bit of orating of *being of sound mind* and *I hereby bequeath*s.

Caps wasn't looking too happy. He was seated opposite Sutton, but the nurse didn't seem to be including him in the chatter. Every now and then he'd glare at me and then at Sutton, giving me an unspoken *Get To It*. Unless I shouted down the table, getting to it would have to wait until after the dessert.

A young man in a dark suit entered, pushing a serving cart before him. This was apparently the guy that Winston had hired to help out, and he was perfection in motion. As he went around the table serving everyone, I found I couldn't take my eyes off him. His height was the only average thing about him. His eyes were deep brown, his face sculpted by a god who knew what he was doing, and his curly black hair called out to me, saying "Come and run your hands through this!" I had to find out his name. I had to find out if he was single. I had to find out if he was gay.

He finally got to me, and his smile made me melt in my chair. "Fish or chicken, sir?" he asked.

"Fishen," I replied.

He chuckled and placed a plate of chicken in front of me before pushing his cart a little farther along and serving Cecily. Everyone else dug in, consuming their food like they hadn't eaten for days, but I couldn't manage to lift my fork until the Vision of Loveliness finished and exited, wheeling his cart with him.

It seemed to me that Cecily had shifted her chair and was sitting uncomfortably close. If I'd been left-handed, I'd have bashed her in the jaw with my elbow every time I tried to cut my meat. I could feel her eyes on me. I'm pretty sure she was mentally undressing me and I could only hope she was getting the proportions right.

My stepmonster's evil stare told me I should do some work, so I forced a smile onto my lips and turned to her. "So," I said, oozing Weasel charm, "you're working on a book about the life of Charlotte Winston?"

"Yes," she replied. "She led a fascinating life. I'm nearly halfway through with the book, and I think it's going to be one of the best biographies of an Illinois luminary to hit the bookshelves."

I thought she was aiming high. After all, there was that Lincoln guy, and he had a fair number of books out on him. Not wanting to rain on her parade, I clicked up the Weasel allure another notch and merely said, "I can't wait to read it."

"If you'd like, after dinner I can read some of it to you."

I wanted to say that I'd rather have fire ants eat my testicles, but I could feel old stepdad's eye on me. "Sounds lovely," I said.

And then I yelped. I've never actually had anyone play footsie with me, but it seemed that Cecily had surreptitiously slipped off her shoe and was running her bare foot up and down my calf.

Several people turned to look at me. Next to me, Ericka looked over her glasses, not sure if she should be concerned at my yelp or irritated. "Are you okay, Mr. Weasley?"

"Fine," I said, my voice rising an octave as Cecily tried slipping her toes up the leg of my jeans.

"You don't seem well," the aunt said. She'd obviously decided I wasn't a good dinner companion.

I wanted to get away from Cecily's probing toes, and I had a safe combination to steal anyway, so I pushed back my chair. "I think I'll excuse myself for a moment, if that's okay."

"The nearest facilities are down the hall, third door on the left," Ericka said helpfully.

I nodded at several people around the table in a way of excusing myself. Cecily smiled at me. "Hurry back," she said. She looked like a cat and had obviously granted me the role of canary.

I left the dining room and quickly made my way upstairs. Caps had pointed out Lawyer Freeman's room to me earlier, but I popped into my own room first. I'd read enough mysteries to know that you didn't just rifle through a stranger's room with your bare hands. I couldn't imagine that Scotland Yard was going to be called in if someone smelled a rat, but just in case, I didn't want my fingerprints all over Freeman's briefcase and notebook.

I put on some black gloves. I was already wearing Nikes, good for sneaking around in, so I was ready. I left my room and headed down the hall.

There seemed to be one hell of a lot of rooms on the second floor. Caps had told me Freeman's was the third door from the end on the north side of the house. I counted, found the door I wanted, and opened it.

The room was deathly quiet. Maybe because I was holding my breath. You know that feeling you get when you know you're doing something that you shouldn't be doing but you're doing it anyway? I felt that if someone were to sneak up behind me and go "Boo" that my heart would say "Fuck it" and just stop beating.

I told myself to think of something else. Think of that gorgeous young man who had served us at dinner. Think of how he'd look naked. Okay, maybe don't think of that. The only thing worse than being found in someone else's room rifling through their things would be to be found in someone else's room pleasuring yourself.

I looked around, my heart racing. There were some suitcases placed next to the bed, but they were empty. Everything had been unpacked. I closed the bedroom door and snapped on the lights. With everyone at dinner, no one would see the light on from outside, and with the sun having set I needed to be able to see what I was doing. I went to the closet and opened it. A bunch of clothes stared back at me. Several pairs of shoes were on the floor. No briefcase. I had expected to see a lot of dark, somber suits, but none was present. Mostly flannel shirts. The shoes weren't Italian leather like the ones currently covering the feet of Lawyer Freeman, either. They were battered basketball shoes and one pair of work boots. Maybe the lawyer, when not doing law, really liked to tone it down and dress like one of the proletariat.

Besides the bed there were a couple of chairs, a dresser, and a desk in the room. I attacked the desk, thinking it would be where a lawyer would put a notebook containing safe combinations and other important notations.

I had just started to examine the contents of the top drawer when the door opened and a very irate Tyler Kendrick entered the room.

Chapter Seven

"WHAT the hell are you doing in here?" he asked, every word dripping with the threat of his fists pounding into my skull.

I slammed the drawer shut quickly and tried to think. My brain refused to cooperate. It finally occurred to me that I could say something along the lines of "I may ask the same thing. What are you doing in Ebert Freeman's room?" but the words got stuck in my throat. All that came out was a sick little gurgle.

Kendrick strode closer. Normally I'm not afraid of people. Thin I may be, but I've got a reputation for being quite a scrapper. I've won out over many a guy who outweighed me by more than a few pounds, mainly because I'm not above cheating. Hey, a good kick in the nuts will stop a bar fight faster than anything. But Tyler Kendrick was no ordinary behemoth. I swear I could see his muscles rippling under his shirt. His fists were clenched and ready. "Come on, Weasel, you little worm. What are you doing in my room?"

His room? I knew I had counted correctly. After all, it's not hard to count to three. The only explanation I could come up with was that Caps didn't know his north from his south. The room I needed was across the hall.

Kendrick looked ready to tear my arms off, so I had to come up with something. My hand was still on the desk drawer, which gave me an idea. "I needed to talk to you. Seeing as you weren't here, I was looking for some notepaper so I could leave you a message."

He came up even closer until our noses were practically touching. Well, he was taller, so my nose was actually closer to his mouth, but you get the idea. I could smell his breath, which was a little sour, like he'd been chomping on tree bark and squirrels all evening. "Why in the hell would you be looking for me?"

It was a good question. I just wished I had an answer to it. I tried to look around him to see if I could make it to the door before he got the chance to pound me with his massive fists, but I couldn't even see around him. He was too close and too bulky. I was foiled by the total eclipse of Kendrick. Escape, therefore, wasn't an option. I had to think of something. Anything.

"My cousin, Kitty, wanted me to leave you a message," I blurted out.

It was the right thing to say, apparently. His face immediately softened and his lips curled at the ends. I think he was attempting to smile. "Really? Kitty wanted to leave me a message?"

"Yes." What the message was, I had no clue. Kendrick was looking at me expectantly, though, so I had to come up with something. "She wants you to call her."

His lip went through more acrobatics in an attempt to look friendly. Honestly, the dude in the Conan Doyle story I was reading would have looked at Kendrick and realized that there were worse things in life than a twisted lip. With horror I realized that Kendrick was actually blushing. "I was going to call her tonight," he said, "but I thought it might be too late. Girls have pretty strict rules about things like that, you know. I thought I'd call her first thing in the morning. She's your cousin, though. Do you think I should go ahead and call her tonight?"

I remembered that I'd given him my cell phone number when I'd been Kitty. I had a vision of him whipping out his phone and punching in my number and then wondering why there was a chirping sound coming from my pocket. "I'd call her tomorrow," I said.

He nodded and backed off a pace from me, allowing me to breathe without taking in Kendrick scent. "So," he said, like we'd been close friends for ages, "she kind of likes me, huh?"

I smiled weakly. "Apparently so."

He put a massive paw on my shoulder. I jumped involuntarily before I realized it was a friendly gesture. "That cousin of yours is some looker. Sorry I came on a little strong just a moment ago, but you know how it is. Finding someone in your room—"

"Understandable," I replied.

"I'll call her first thing in the morning," he said. He all but shuffled his feet shyly and muttered, "Gosh!"

"Not too early. Girls like their beauty sleep." I made a mental note to check all incoming calls and answer with the appropriate voice. I'd have to make sure Kendrick's call didn't go to my voice mail. When he heard my voice saying to leave a message, even an idiot like Kendrick might catch on that he'd been had.

Kendrick looked over my shoulder. "My closet door is open. I was sure I'd closed it."

"The place is supposed to be haunted. Perhaps Great-granddad Winston was in here, searching for the other half of his face. He lost part of it in World War Two, or so I'm to understand."

Kendrick frowned. "You talk weird, Weasel."

"I suppose it's all those British mysteries I read. I like to keep my mind occupied."

The big guy shrugged. "I always just thought it was because you were a fruit, but Jake Winston's gay as hell and he talks normal."

Stephen Osborne

There was an awkward pause. You know how it is when you're talking with someone that you don't like to speak to and you've covered the weather and how it's been a shitty day so far but things are looking up and then you don't have a single thing to say? We'd reached that point. Still, the behemoth was standing between me and the door and he wasn't shifting. "Well," I said.

"Yes," he replied.

"I suppose now that I've relayed my message, I ought to be getting along. Things to do, you know."

Enlightenment dawned in Kendrick's excuse for a brain and he moved aside. "Don't let me keep you. Thanks for delivering Kitty's message, Weasel."

I breathed a sigh of relief as I hit the door. It occurred to me that I needed to add one more thing to my weekend list, the one that included setting Caps up with Keith Sutton and nudging Cecily Talbot over to the Dollings author list. Now I had five: Answer phone call from Kendrick in my Kitty voice.

Out in the hall, people were shuffling around, going into bedrooms. I'd spent too much time in the wrong room, and now dinner was over. It was too late to ransack the lawyer's room as he might come in at any moment. I decided to find Caps and tell him that he was an idiot for not knowing simple directions and to inform him that I'd given my best and now it was all up to him. I was washing my hands of the will swap. There was enough on my plate as it was.

Caps's Aunt Ericka was emerging from what I assumed was her room. She paused to look down her nose at me. I was taller, so she had to tilt her head back to do it, but I guess it was important enough to her to make the effort. "You missed the rest of dinner, Mr. Weasley."

"I suppose I did. Sorry about that."

"I hope you're not feeling ill?"

I just had Tyler Kendrick thank me, so my stomach was a little sour. Therefore I replied truthfully. "Some stomach troubles. I'm better now."

She sniffed. "Some of us are meeting downstairs for bridge in the recreation room. I believe some of the men are going to the billiard room to play pool, if you prefer that."

The place had a billiard room? Was I in a giant version of the board game *Clue*? I bet if I searched around I'd find a conservatory, a library, and a study. I just had to make sure I didn't end up the dead body, killed by Mr. Green (Kendrick) in the hall with the candlestick.

I nipped downstairs, thinking I'd find Caps in the billiard room. I didn't exactly know where the room was, so I had to do a bit of searching. I found the recreation room with no trouble, where my stepmonster and loads of others were gathering around tables ready for playing bridge. Dollings was maneuvering himself so that he would be seated next to Cecily Talbot. I managed to get out of the room without him seeing me. I was sure he'd want me to join them and extol the virtues of Dollings Press to Cecily, and I wanted no part of it. Bridge bores me. Euchre is my game.

I opened several more doors until I finally came across the billiard room. There was only one occupant, though. Standing by the window, chalking his cue, was Keith Sutton. He flashed me a smile. "You're Jake's friend, aren't you?"

"That's me. Pat Weasley, but everyone calls me Weasel."

"I thought Mr. Winston was going to challenge me to a game, but he had to attend to something in the kitchen. Maybe you'd like a game?"

I was a fairly good pool player, and it would give me the opportunity to scratch number one off my list, so I nodded. "Be glad to."

He insisted that I break, so I grabbed a cue and sent the cue ball smacking into the bevy of colored balls. When the dust settled, I was solids, having sunk the one ball. To get the conversation rolling, I asked, "Have you been here long? Staying at the house, I mean. Not here in the billiard room. I know you haven't been in here long, because everyone just finished with dinner. Is there a conservatory, do you know? Maybe a ballroom?"

He chuckled at my nervous rambling. "I'm not sure which question I should answer first, so I'll just go with the first. I've been living here for about a year. I came shortly after Mrs. Winston became ill. And no, there's no conservatory or ballroom."

"Shame," I said, muffing a shot. "This seems like a real-life *Clue* house otherwise. Is there a secret panel behind the bookcase in the library at least?"

"Afraid not," he said, sinking in one of his balls. As he set up his next shot, he asked, "So you're in college?"

"Rockford College. I was at Purdue University, but I got thrown out. Therefore I was commanded to return to the homestead so that my mother and stepmonster can keep a closer eye on me."

His eyes twinkled at me. "You look like the type that knows how to get himself into trouble."

"It doesn't seem to be a difficulty with me." It occurred to me that I should be starting to extol the virtues of Caps to this admittedly fine-looking young nurse, but finding a way to broach the subject was proving a problem. Finally an idea struck me as Sutton missed his shot and it was my turn. I knocked in another one of my balls and said, "This house is a bit remote. Seems like it would be pretty lonely out here."

"It's quiet, that's for sure."

"Are you single?" I asked, lining up my next shot. "If that's not being too forward."

Sutton smiled easily. "At present I am."

"Me, too. Even with a whole college full of young hotties, it's sort of hard to find just the right one to settle down with." I thought of McCaffrey and the fun that I might have had with him. It still was fuzzy in my head. "Mind you, searching for that right one can be fun."

Sutton gave me a sly smile. I think he knew what I was leading up to. "Sometimes, though, you don't have to be looking, do you? I mean, sometimes the perfect person just shows up out of nowhere, when you least expect it."

"Exactly!" I paused to put a little extra chalk on my stick. "And then there are those who are too shy to say anything themselves. They can't put their feelings into the proper words themselves, so they have to get someone else to pave the way, so to speak."

"Or they wait for the other guy to make the first move," Sutton said. He gave me a furtive glance. "I hope I'm not being too forward, but you are gay, right?"

"Got my membership card years ago."

He laughed. "I just wanted to make sure my gaydar was working correctly. I hate it when you think you're reading signals correctly only to find you've got everything wrong."

I thought of Kendrick and his crush on the nonexistent Kitty Wells. "It can lead to trouble," I agreed.

Sutton leaned against his cue stick. "So am I right in thinking that there's someone in the house that's interested in me? Someone too shy to make the first move?"

I beamed at him. It was nice to meet someone so quick on the uptake. "Exactly what I'm trying to convey."

I had to lean across the table a bit to get the angle I wanted. Sutton was standing near the corner where I was, but he didn't move far to get out of my way. In fact, he moved a few paces back but then brushed up against my butt. "And this person is just waiting for me to make the first move, huh?"

His words were on the right track, but it was hard to think with his leg brushed up against my rear. I took the shot and missed. "Um, right," I said, straightening.

Stephen Osborne

Sutton spun me around, his arms around me. "Sometimes they pop up when you least expect them, don't they?" he said. "I've seen the way you've been looking at me. I just want you to know that I think you're hot, too."

And he planted a kiss right on my lips.

Now, I want to be clear on this: if I had been giving this Sutton looks, it was only at dinner, and then only to ensure I had the right guy in mind so that I could talk to him about Caps. It would have been disastrous, not to mention wrong on every level, to have gotten the guy wrong and tried to set Caps up with his cousin Charlie or someone like that. I also want it to be known that I didn't kiss back. I was in shock. And, yes, my hands went up and around him, but in preparation for pushing him away and ending the lip-lock. Unfortunately, just as my arms wrapped around him, the door opened and Caps entered.

Chapter Eight

I DID what most people would do in this situation. I jumped back quickly. Unfortunately, this only makes you look as guilty as a kid caught with his hand in the cookie jar. It was the John Adair business all over again. I could feel the heat in my cheeks as I sputtered, "It isn't what you think."

Caps eyed me coldly. "No?"

"No!" I managed a weak smile. "You see, I was talking with Keith here—"

"It didn't look like talking."

Sutton placed his cue stick back in the rack on the wall, the game apparently over. He frowned at Caps. "Were you looking for someone?" he asked my friend, not bothering to hide his annoyance.

"I was checking up on Weasel here. Little did I know just how much he needed checking up on."

"There's an explanation for this, you know," I said. I tried a laugh. It didn't come out too well. More like having a lump of phlegm caught in your throat than a devil-may-care chuckle.

"I suppose," Caps said, letting the sarcasm drip, "that you're going to tell me that you were choking on a bit of food and that Keith was attempting to dislodge it with his tongue."

"No," I said. "That would be silly. You see, what happened was—"

It seemed no one was going to let me get the explanation out. This time Sutton interrupted me. "It's really none of your business what happened, Winston. Perhaps you'd let us get on with our game."

Caps sniffed. "I'll let you get on with whatever you want." He stepped out into the hall and began to close the door behind him. "You might," he added glumly, "want to lock the door if you're going to end up doing it on the pool table. Aunt Ericka might enjoy watching two guys getting it on, but I don't think that Weasel's stepfather would enjoy seeing his stepson writhing in ecstasy with another dude."

There seemed to be to be a veiled threat behind those words. Under normal circumstances, Caps wouldn't rat me out to Dollings for all the money in the world. However, Caps was one of those All's Fair in Love and War sorts, and while I didn't think he'd go tattling to the step-padre, I felt it was best to go after him and explain before he had the chance. I therefore made for the door, telling Sutton, "I'd better go after him."

"See you later, then," the nurse said as I legged it out into the hall. I only half registered the words in my brain. I was trying to decide which way to go. To the left I'd find Dollings and the others playing cards. To the right I could go up the stairs to Caps's room. I went right.

And bumped into the cute guy who had served us at dinner.

"Sorry," he said, blushing so adorably that I liked him even more. "Wasn't watching where I was going."

"My fault," I replied truthfully. "I was in a hurry. You didn't see Caps go this way, by any chance?"

"Caps?"

"You'd know him as Jake Winston, the nephew of the owner of the house."

"Oh," he said, understanding dawning. "As a matter of fact, he just went upstairs. He looked pretty angry."

"Bit of a mix-up. Right now he probably wants to break my leg." I put out my hand by way of introduction. I needed to find out this guy's name. "I'm Patrick Weasley, but everyone calls me Weasel."

"Weasel," he repeated with a smile. "I like that. I'm Tony. Tony Turner."

I amped up the charm. I figured since Caps hadn't made a beeline for my stepdad that I was safe at least for a little while. I could talk to him later and straighten things out, but for now I could get to know the beautiful Tony. "Nice to meet you," I said as we shook hands.

"So, why does Jake want to break your leg?"

"Long story."

Tony's smile turned into a shy one. "I was just heading to the kitchen for a nightcap before heading to bed. Maybe you'd like to join me and tell me all about it?" He flushed when he realized what he'd said. "I meant to join me for a drink, not to bed. I wouldn't be that forward."

I would. But I didn't want to scare him off, so I merely said, "I'd love to join you for a drink."

We made our way to the kitchen, where we settled around a dining table that would have had size envy issues if it had been introduced to the table residing in the dining room. The cook, a Mrs. Donleavy, was just finishing up the dishes as we arrived and declined our offer to join us for a drink. "It's getting late," she said, grabbing her coat. "I'd best be getting home. You're staying here overnight, I understand, Tony?" She said it with a sly look in her eyes.

"Yeah. Thought I'd stay here for the weekend. Save going back and forth from town."

"Well," Mrs. Donleavy said, eyes darting from him to me and back again. "Try and get a little sleep. We'll have a big day tomorrow. Don't want you falling asleep as you're serving the soup."

After she'd departed by the kitchen exit, Tony busied himself with getting us each a vodka and tonic. He tried to keep his back to me to mask his embarrassment, but I could see his reflection in a mirror over the sideboard where he was mixing the concoctions. The boy was positively crimson. "Mrs. Donleavy watches too many romantic movies. She's always trying to play matchmaker."

I suspected Mrs. Donleavy had read the situation accurately and had hastened her departure to allow Tony and me to be alone. I liked that in a woman. "She seems nice," I said.

His blush had faded only slightly as he turned and handed me my drink. "Mrs. Donleavy likes to think she looks after me." He sat down catty-corner to me, which made me happy. If he'd sat opposite me, it wouldn't have been as easy to gaze into his deep brown eyes. He seemed to be having trouble making eye contact, though. I'd have to ease the shyness out of him.

We chatted amiably. I learned that he was indeed gay and even better—single. Mind you, I had to coax that info out of him. He was more relaxed when talking about his home life. He lived with his two brothers in the nearby town of Shannon. He didn't go out to bars much and didn't like dance music (I could live with that), didn't read mysteries (I could work on that), and had never bowled in his life (I'd have to change that). He'd been recommended for the job of butler/server for the weekend by Mrs. Donleavy, who was the usual cook for the Winstons. He was twenty-three and wanted to be a singer. "Right now I'm working part-time at an auto parts store. I've been thinking about trying out for some of the musicals in Chicago, though. Maybe I can get a small part or something. You never know." He paused, and the blush came back. "Here I am hogging the conversation, though. You were going to tell me about Jake and why he was mad at you."

Warmed by the vodka and Tony's eyes, I'd forgotten about Caps entirely. While he got us seconds on our drinks, I related the tale of me and Caps and the nurse, Sutton. Naturally I stressed the more humorous elements of the story, as I didn't want to alarm Tony. When I finished my tale, he shook his head and chuckled.

"Would it be so bad if Jake did tell your stepfather? I mean, he's going to find out someday, isn't he?"

"I'd like to put that day off as long as possible. You saw the guy at dinner. He's Satan without the horns. Hitler used to get advice on how to be nasty from him."

Tony laughed. "I'm sure Jake—Caps—will understand as soon as you explain things to him."

"We've been friends for ages. He'll laugh when I tell him it was all a misunderstanding." I frowned. "Mind you, I don't think I'm going to be successful in getting him and Sutton together."

"No, I don't think so, either!" With another laugh, Tony looked over at the clock on the wall. "God, I hadn't realized how long we've been chatting. I didn't mean to keep you so long."

"I've enjoyed it."

His eyes twinkled. "Fishen," he said.

"Pardon?"

"That's the first thing you said to me, when I asked you if you wanted fish or chicken. I thought it was cute."

Now it was my turn to blush. "Well," I admitted, "it was hard to think with those dark eyes of yours looking at me."

Once again he was unable to look me in the face. God, he was so shy and so cute. And older than me, which made the shyness and cuteness even more endearing. "I'd better get to bed," he said. "I didn't mean to keep you up so long."

It wasn't quite midnight, which was pretty much when my nights usually got going. I made a decision. Sometimes if you let shy types go at their own pace, they got gun shy and didn't do anything. So I figured I'd force things along. "Going to bed?" I asked. "Alone?"

That made him stammer a bit. "Well... yeah. I mean... yeah. I don't—"

"I just thought we could get to know each other better. We don't have to do anything, but I enjoy talking with you and don't want this to end."

"Shouldn't you go and square things with your friend?" His gaze was on a spot on the table, and his face couldn't get redder. I could tell he was scared but tempted.

"Tell you what. I'll go and talk with Caps if you agree to come to my room in an hour's time."

Tony grinned shyly and put his hand, which was shaking slightly, on mine. "It's a deal."

IT WAS with a glad heart that I took the steps up to the second floor two at a time. And why not? I was going to set things right with Caps, and I had a fun romp between the sheets to look forward to. What could be better? Although it was late, I knew Caps would still be up. Like me, he was a night owl.

To prove my point, when I got up to the second floor hall, I spotted Caps just a few doors down, coming out of his bedroom. I called to him. He turned, saw me, and bunched his skinny shoulders.

"Now, Caps, old friend, you need to under—"

He charged, emitting a war cry as he barreled down the corridor. Now I knew what the big-game hunters of yore felt when the rhinos had enough of their company and decided to run at them. Granted, this was a pretty skinny rhino and he didn't have a horn, but the charge was similar. Caps was faster than I gave him credit for as well. I had time to put my hands up in protection and that was about it. His head hit me square in the chest, and the two of us crashed to the carpet.

We rolled as he flailed his arms about, trying to hit me. Under normal circumstances I wouldn't consider Caps to be a difficult opponent. He wasn't much of a scrapper, but his anger was fueling unknown depths, plus I wasn't fighting back, only trying to block his punches.

"Really," I managed to say as we rolled and he was temporarily under me, "if you'd just—"

He yelled his battle cry again and somehow managed to shift me off him. He clung to me like a shirt that had just come out of the dryer, and once again we rolled. This time, though, as I fell back, there didn't seem to be floor to roll onto, only air. We'd hit the stairs. Suddenly my back hit a step, and I yelped. Momentum carried us and we rolled down the stairs, locked in our embrace. Caps's war cry changed to a couple of *Ow*s and *Ouch*es and I believe I may have given out an *Argghh* or two and a few *Shit*s. I hit my head against the wall at least once. We hit the landing, and you would have thought that Caps would have released his grasp and we could have taken inventory of the damages, but he retained his grip and even attempted to throttle me. I tried to pull back from him, and we ended up tumbling down the rest of the stairs to the main floor. This time we didn't go sideways, but fell head over heels like a circus tumbling act. It was murder on the noggin, not to mention the back. Come to think of it, the arms and legs didn't enjoy it much, either. I've taken worse spills. One skateboarding incident when I was fourteen that left my right arm in a Z shape comes to mind. Still, on a scale of one to ten this was definitely a solid nine. We finally hit the floor, and Caps went flying, knocking into a small table and causing a vase to fall off and crash to the ground.

Naturally the ruckus came to the attention of most, if not all, of the house party. I heard people coming down the stairs, and someone asked, "What in the world is going on?" The bridge game must have still been in full swing, as a gaggle of card players, including Dollings and Cecily, came out of the recreation room. Cecily screamed. The stepmonster demanded to know what I thought I was doing, although I thought that should have been obvious.

I groaned and tried to get up. My head was woozy and the first attempt was unsuccessful, and I only made it to my knees before collapsing. I reached up and caught hold of something and used that to haul myself up. It was only when I got to my feet that I realized I'd grabbed hold of Keith Sutton's belt. It was a good thing Caps was still lying there with his eyes closed, rubbing his head, or he might have charged again, seeing me with my hand at Sutton's crotch.

Sutton steadied me, and Cecily came running up and took up position on the opposite side. Between them I managed to stay on my feet. "I'm okay," I said. This wasn't technically true, as I felt like I'd just had a tussle with Mike Tyson in his prime, but I meant okay as in all the extremities seemed to be unbroken. I wasn't sure about the head. The eyesight wasn't doing so well, either, as there seemed to be too many Suttons, Dollingses, and Cecilys.

"Oh, you poor dear," one of the Cecilys said.

I think I smiled at her before I passed out.

I LATER learned that I was only out a few minutes, but when I opened my eyes, I was disoriented and panicked, thinking I'd died or was in the hospital or at the Republican National Convention, because I raised my head with a start and cried out.

I was in the bed that had been reserved for me in the Winston home. Someone had taken off my shoes, but otherwise I was still clothed. Cecily was on one side of the bed, looking concerned. She smiled. "So… yes?" She was holding my hand.

I vaguely knew that I'd said something to her and suspected that we'd exchanged several sentences, but my brain still wasn't working and I spoke without the words actually registering. I had no idea what

I was yessing to, but I nodded. I regretted the nod immediately as it caused my brain to gasp and yell *Whoa*.

The door opened and Sutton entered, toting a small black duffel bag that turned out to be his stash of pills, wraps, bandages, and whatnot. I was up on my elbows and he gently forced me back so that my head once again met the pillow.

"Hold on there, slugger," he said with a wry smile. He took a little penlight out of his pocket and shone it into my eyes. I blinked. "You sustained a slight concussion. You're lucky. You could have broken your silly neck doing a stunt like that."

My eyes darted around the room, looking for a clock. "What time is it?" I asked, a hint of desperation in my tone.

"Relax. You've just been out a minute or two. I wanted to send for an ambulance, but your stepfather insisted that wasn't necessary. I'd recommend you stay in bed for now, and I'll check you in the morning to make sure you're okay. We'll see then if you need to be checked out in the emergency room."

Actually, it wasn't my condition that made me worry about lost time. I was worried about missing my tryst with the delectable Tony. At my age, horny wins out over battered and concussed. I just hoped my head ceased to throb by the time he arrived.

"I think I'll be fine," I said. "Just have a little headache."

Sutton fussed around for several more minutes, pressing his fingers against my head and asking, "Does it hurt here?" and making me bend my arms and wiggle my toes. Satisfied that I wasn't ready for a full body cast and traction, he picked up his bag. "You'll live," he announced. "I'd better go down the hall and check out your sparring partner." He paused near the door to wink at me. The wink spoke volumes. It was an "I'm not finished with you, my cute Weasel" wink if I ever saw one.

After he'd gone, Cecily continued to hold my hand. "I'll stay with you, if you like. Until you fall asleep, I mean."

I had no intention of sleeping, nor did I want her in my room when Tony came knocking at my door. "I'll be okay," I insisted. "You go on back down and finish the card game."

That made her laugh. "Only you would think of other people's entertainment after suffering a fall like that. You're a marvel." She leaned over and gave me a peck on the cheek. "It'll be hard, seeing your stepfather and not telling him our news, but I think we should wait until we're together, don't you?"

I had no idea what she was talking about, and I worried for a moment that my sore skull had been battered more than I'd thought, but I wanted her out of the room, so I just replied, "Sure."

Before she left she gave me another little kiss on the cheek, which I thought was odd. Still, I breathed a sigh of relief when the door closed behind her, and I slowly raised my head, swung my legs off the bed, and stood. I was happy to learn that my legs still knew how to hold up the rest of my body. I took a few steps. Walking was stiff, but not quite at Frankenstein's monster levels, so that was good. As long as we didn't get too acrobatic, I could survive a romp with Tony.

My room didn't have its own bathroom, so I had to go down the hall to prepare. I brushed my teeth and ran a hand through my hair and checked myself in the mirror. There was a slight cut below my left eye that Sutton had bandaged and a big purple bruise coming into the picture on my right bicep, but other than that I looked pretty good. I returned to my room and waited for Tony.

It wasn't a long wait. I'd barely turned on my Kindle and gotten back into my Holmes story before there was a light tap at the door. "Come on in," I said.

The door opened slowly and Tony entered, looking nervous and excited in equal amounts. "Hey," he said.

"Hey," I replied.

He closed the door behind him, trying not to make much noise. "I figured everyone would be asleep by now." He hovered by the door, as if afraid to approach the bed. I wasn't going to eat him. Well, not literally.

"No, the place still seems to be hopping."

"No one saw me come here, though," he said, as if to reassure me.

"As long as my stepfather doesn't see you, I don't care if you send out event invitations on Facebook," I said.

He took a tentative step. "I'm not used to this sort of thing," he said shyly.

I put the Kindle aside and got out of bed. Going over to him, I pulled him close and kissed him gently on the lips. "It'll be okay," I said. "We can take things slow. We won't do anything you don't want to do."

It could be that he wanted to do quite a lot, because he suddenly grasped my face with both hands and attacked my tonsils with his tongue. Or maybe he just wanted to warm his tongue. The oral blitzkrieg caught me by surprise—after all, he'd been giving me the Oh I'm Shy and Inexperienced act—and since my legs still weren't up to 100 percent, I fell back. Luckily the bed was there. We stumbled, hit, and bounced a little, all the time trying to pull off each other's clothes.

He broke off the kiss long enough to moan and say, "You're so beautiful." I flipped him off me and dove on top of him, fumbling with the buttons of his shirt. Soon it was raining garments as pants, socks, and underwear went flying. Somehow we got under the covers and the kissing continued as our hands went exploring. I liked what they found. We stroked each other and my tongue did a molar count in his mouth. All were present and accounted for. He smiled without a pause in the kissing. When I eventually pulled my lips off his, he said, "Do you have lube and condoms?"

"Like the Boy Scouts, I come prepared. Never travel without them." There was a short pause in the carnal action as I had to get out of bed to get my stash of sex-time necessities, but I quickly returned, partly because I wanted to get back to the action and partly because it was a little chilly in the room. I suppose it's not easy to heat a house that size without going into debt. I flicked out the lights and then got back under the covers, and our lips reacquainted themselves. We groped and fondled some more, and then I slipped on a condom and lubed up the old pole. Tony grinned as I raised his legs up to my shoulders, somehow keeping the covers over my back. If I was going to shake, it was going to be for the right reasons and not because the room was cold.

"Start off slow," he whispered.

I promised I would, although looking into his eyes, which showed as mere black pools in the meager light coming in from the window, it wasn't going to be easy. I wanted to devour him. Being the sweet and gentle lover, though, I swallowed hard and slowly began to enter him.

He hissed and then moaned softly.

I was about to say *Oh, baby* or *Wow* or *That feels so good* or words to that effect when I heard a heavy foot tread outside my door. I barely had time to move before the door was thrown open with force and I heard my stepfather's growl.

"Patrick Carrington Weasley!" he thundered.

Chapter Nine

I DIDN'T have time to actually think, so I just acted. Tony's legs were quickly thrown down and I collapsed on top of him, hiding him as much as I could with my body. I held my breath. Tony let out a tiny gasp as my body weight slammed on top of him, but otherwise he was silent.

I didn't dare look over at the doorway, but I could hear Dollings fumbling about. "Where's the damned light switch?"

"Don't turn the lights on!" I said.

"Why not?"

I didn't dare move, even though bony bits of Tony were jabbing me awkwardly. I could sense Tony holding in his breath. Smart guy. He had quickly realized just how dire the situation was. What I couldn't believe, going by the fact that Daddy Dollings hadn't exploded into thirteen billion pieces, was that the stepmonster hadn't realized I was lying on top of someone. True, the room was pretty dark, but still. "You know how it is when you've been in the dark, snoozing away. You'll blind me," I said.

"You'll get used to it."

I turned my head to look in his direction, which may have been a good thing to do, in that my head at least partially obscured Tony's face. With any luck, in the dim light, Dollings might just think it was a shadow or something. "Forget the lights," I said. "What is it that's so important that you burst into my room like this?"

"I wanted to talk with you, and to see if you were all right after your fall. Why are you lying like that with your butt up in the air?"

Well, you try lying flat when someone's lying under you, especially when you didn't have time to arrange all the bits and pieces. One of Tony's legs didn't make it all the way down and was twisted under me, his knee gouging my groin. To be fair, the position probably was no more comfortable for Tony and he wasn't complaining. He was doing his best not to breathe.

"Leg cramp," I said lamely.

"Well, you look weird." I could see his dark form still searching for the lights. His hand was getting perilously close to the switch.

"If you want to have a chat," I said quickly, "why don't I meet you downstairs in a minute or so? Hard to talk to you like this, you know, since I sleep nude and all that. Feels a bit creepy, being naked and talking with my stepfather with only a thin sheet separating my unclothed state and your eyes."

I couldn't actually make out the details of his face, but I could hear the frown in his tone. "You mean you sleep without any clothes on?"

"Au naturel."

The stepmonster puffed. "Very well. I certainly can't talk with you like this. Are you sure you can make it downstairs, though? That nurse fellow seemed to think you should stay in bed and rest."

"I'm fine. Honestly."

"Very well. I'll be in the study. Don't keep me waiting." Still he hesitated. "What were you doing when I came in?"

"Doing?" I asked.

"Yes. You were making odd sounds. That's why I shouted. I wanted you to stop."

"Um, I was groaning. The pain, you know. From the fall."

"Well, it sounded very strange."

"It was a really good fall."

This seemed to satisfy him. He closed the door behind him, and Tony and I breathed a simultaneous sigh of relief. I rolled off of him and tried to get my heart rate back down to normal.

"I can't believe," Tony said finally, "that he didn't see that I was under you."

"Luckily for us there's not much of a moon tonight and we were pretty much in shadow. If he'd have found the light switch, though, I don't think I could have easily talked my way out of that one." I grabbed his hand and gave it a little squeeze. "Sorry about that."

He laughed that laugh you give when you realize the hurricane has come and gone and you're still alive and kicking. "No problem. It does feel good to stretch out my leg, though, I can tell you that."

"Yeah, your knee was rammed right up into my 'nads."

"I'm sorry."

"They'll live. They've gone through worse. Some incidents with bicycle seats when I was a kid come to mind."

Tony laughed again and rubbed a hand over his face. "Oh, my God, I can't believe we got away with that. What was that he said about you having a fall, though? Are you hurt? I noticed you have a bandage by your eye."

"I took the express down the stairs earlier. I'm fine. A few bruises."

I could make out the twinkle in his eyes. "Want me to kiss them and make them better?"

I sighed and hauled myself out of the bed. "I'd love it, but it'll have to keep. Jasper K. Dollings doesn't like waiting, and if I don't get down there soon, he'll be back up here, and this time he might find the light switch." I leaned over and planted a kiss on Tony's soft, lovely lips. "Will you wait for me?"

He smiled. "You bet, tiger!"

It took a minute or two to locate all of my clothes, especially since after each item found, I paused to lock lips with Tony. Eventually I was dressed. At the door I stopped and blew him a kiss. "Be back as soon as I can."

"I'll be waiting."

It may have been the adrenaline from the idea of getting laid, but my head no longer throbbed. My body, however, wasn't at peak performance, especially going down stairs. I had to grip the hand rail, and even then I said *Ouch* every third step as a bolt of pain shot through my battered legs.

I was glad when I was on level ground again. There was no noise coming from the recreation room, so I figured the card game had finally dispersed. In fact, no one was in sight. This was a bit of a shame, as it would have been useful to be able to ask someone just where this study was. Mark Winston had pointed it out when we'd first arrived as we'd made our way to the library, but I couldn't recall just where it was. Tumbling down stairs headfirst will do that to you. I began opening doors, hoping the study would be close and I wouldn't have to try too many.

Three doors down I found success. Room with books and a big old desk, containing one stepfather. Dollings, worryingly, had a smile on his face when he turned and saw me coming in. He was over by the sideboard, pouring himself a drink.

"Come in, come in," he said, although I had already done so. He sounded positively jovial, which added to my trepidation. "Would you like a drink? Our host said we could help ourselves, and I believe this is a cause for celebration."

I nodded cautiously. Drinking after a mild concussion probably wasn't the wisest thing to do, but the stepmonster was scaring me with his smile and his hearty nature. I'd never seen him in such a state. I looked behind a chair or two to see if there were alien pods about that had replaced Dollings with a rather bad copy.

"Sit down, Patrick," he said, handing me a glass. "You're a vodka man, if I remember correctly."

He'd made me an Absolut and tonic. I sipped it cautiously, expecting it to be laced with strychnine. It tasted okay. I sat down but kept myself braced. I knew that any moment he was going to revert to his true self and start ranting and yelling, and I wanted to be prepared for a dash to the door. Dollings sat down opposite me, something on his face that on another person would be described as a smile.

"You've surprised me, I have to admit," he said, raising his glass to toast me. "You've succeeded beyond my wildest expectations."

Ah. Now things made sense. If I'd succeeded, although I had no idea how I did so, it must have transpired that Cecily Talbot agreed to publish her horrid little tome with Dollings Press. Maybe she felt sorry for me after my fall. I did recall exchanging a few words with her upon awaking which were lost in the mists of my brain. That must have been when she agreed.

I took another sip. The vodka did seem to ease my aching muscles. I crossed my legs and said airily, "It was nothing."

"Nothing, he says." My stepfather took a healthy dose of his own drink. "Honestly, I can't believe you did it. I knew that young Talbot amazingly had her sights fixed on you, but I really didn't think you could get her to come over to Dollings Press. Having you come this weekend was a last ditch effort on my part, but it paid off."

I waved a dismissive hand. "All part of the Weasley service." I took a drink.

"And to get engaged to the girl, now that's something I really didn't expect."

I sputtered, spraying out vodka and tonic. After coughing a few times, I managed to croak out a question. "What?"

Dollings grinned. "I know. She wasn't supposed to tell anyone until the two of you had a chance to make the announcement together, but she couldn't help but spill the good news. Congratulations, my boy. She'll make you a fine wife."

I set my drink aside. There must be something in the tonic water that caused auditory hallucinations. "Wife?"

The stepmonster continued beaming. "I'm really pleased. To be perfectly frank, since you haven't shown any interest in women since I married your mother and you're always hanging out with those odd friends of yours, I was beginning to worry that you might be... well, I thought that you might be homosexual." He laughed as if that was the biggest joke he'd heard all day.

"There must be some mistake," I said weakly.

"Oh, I owe you an apology, that's for sure. Nothing worse than someone thinking you could be one of... them." Dollings curled his lip in disgust. "And I should have known better. No stepson of mine could be a fruit, after all! But, like I said, the thought crossed my mind. Those weird friends of yours and the lack of female companionship. I should have seen that you were just waiting for the right girl. And you've found her! I couldn't be happier!"

"Engaged?" What the hell had I said after I'd come out of my concussed state? It had seemed to me just a few mumbled words, but apparently it had been enough conversation to not only convince Cecily to publish with my stepdad but also to marry me. I had to find Cecily at the earliest convenience and set her straight.

Dollings chuckled and rose. I thought he was going to refresh his now empty glass, but he came over to my chair and patted me on the shoulder. I admit I flinched when he touched me, expecting him to club me about the face and neck as usual. But no—friendly tap. Much scarier.

"You've made me a very happy man tonight, Patrick," he said. "I can't wait to let your mother in on the news in the morning. As you know, we are the guardians of your trust fund. Your father wasn't the wisest man, perhaps, but he knew that you would take longer to mature than most men, so he ensured that your money would be looked after responsibly. You get it in any case when you turn twenty-five, but I think I can convince your mother that we should release it on your wedding day." More laughing and shoulder patting. "Not that I'm encouraging you to have a short engagement! No, indeed. Enjoy this time, my boy!"

I blinked. It was a hell of a lot of money. But *No No No No No*. I couldn't, not for all the money in the world. I doubted if the stepmonster would make the same offer if I was getting hitched to Tony or some other lovely male.

Tony, who was still up in my room. I had to get back up there. I rose, my legs shaky this time not from the fall but from the news I'd just received. "I have to get back up to my room," I said. "Rest and all that. The tumble took a lot out of me."

"Yes, yes, I didn't mean to keep you. Just wanted to tell you how proud I am. You get some rest. Big day tomorrow. You and Cecily get to make your announcement, and then there's the reading of that will Sunday night. I expect that dear Charlotte didn't forget how kind I've always been to her."

The man already had more money than anyone needed, and here he was hoping he'd get a nice chunk of Charlotte's bounty. I don't know which churned my stomach more, his avarice or his newfound chumminess toward me.

I left the study like a somnambulist. I had nearly made the stairs before I realized that someone was trying to get my attention by making "pssst" sounds. I turned to see Mark Winston's head poking out of a doorway. He signaled for me to enter.

The room turned out to be the library. Still thinking of *Clue*, I examined the room, wondering where the secret passage was located. I decided that the section of bookcase behind the desk swung open to reveal a dark tunnel. Winston didn't seem interested in secret passages, though. His brow was furrowed with worry as he made sure the door was securely closed behind us. That done, he got straight to business.

"The combination! Do you have it?" he asked.

I was engaged to a woman I could barely stand to be in the same room with and I had a hot young man up in my bed. The last thing on my mind was that stupid combination and that stupid will. I shook my head. "Due to the inability of your nephew to point out the right bedroom, I was unable to get the combination. Caps will have to perform both functions, combination pilfering and will swapping. Sorry."

Winston emitted a moan and placed a hand on the wall for support. He looked like a man on the verge of collapse. "But... Jake can't do anything! He's confined to his bed after that fall down the stairs! That nurse my wife engaged gave him some powerful painkillers, and he's pretty much out of it! I don't think he could manage to put on his pants correctly, let alone perform a simple little will swap!"

I shrugged. I felt sorry for Caps, of course, but the tumble had been his fault. For my part, I'd done what I could for Winston, who was a nice dude and better than most of my relatives. "Well, let's be honest. What we were planning was illegal anyway. If your wife wanted Kendrick to get some of her money—"

"Nearly a million dollars," Winston said, shaking his head. "I won't get much, not with the present will. Not enough to keep this house. I'll have to sell it and get a tiny little apartment."

A million dollars, for a cheap fuck like Kendrick? Either Charlotte had gone off her rocker or Kendrick was hung like a horse or just one hell of a good lay. "Wow," was all I could say.

Winston gazed into my face, his eyes pleading. "I don't suppose that you—"

"No," I said firmly. "I'm sorry."

He sighed heavily. "I suppose I'll either have to do it myself, then, or just resign myself to losing the house."

"I have to point out," I said, "that by now Lawyer Freeman is snuggled in his bed, snoozing away. You'd have to sneak into his room while he was in there. The chances of you getting away with such a scheme are slim and none."

He arched an eyebrow at me. "I could get him down here on some pretext and then you could—"

"No, I couldn't."

"Jake would be disappointed in you."

I could see the man was desperate, but I remained resolute. "The last time I saw Caps, he headbutted me in the chest, sending us down the stairs the hard way."

"Is that what caused the two of you to act like an alcoholic acrobatic team? Why on earth did he headbutt you?"

"He'd just seen me kissing the nurse, Sutton."

Winston frowned. "I wouldn't have thought that would anger my nephew. He generally likes seeing boys kiss other boys."

"He's got his heart set on this Sutton guy. He thought I was making advances on his intended, so to speak."

"Well, if you were kissing the guy, I can see where he might get that impression."

"All a mistake. Sutton snogged me. I didn't snog back."

"You should have told Jake that he got a mistaken impression."

"I tried. It's hard to say much when you're flying down steps head over heels."

Winston chewed his lip. "I think," he said slowly, "that we need to go up and see Jake. He'll sleep better knowing that he was mistaken about you."

I hesitated. While I wanted more than anything to make amends with Caps, I had Tony waiting for me. Still, if Caps was hurt enough to warrant painkillers, I needed to do my bit to ease his mental pain, at least. I could give him a quick apology and we'd have a good chuckle and I could be back up in my bed with Tony's legs around my shoulders in no time.

"Lead the way," I said.

In retrospect, I did notice a little gleam in Winston's eye as we went up to Caps's room. At the time I just thought he was happy to bring two chums back together, but it turned out his devious mind was plotting.

Chapter Ten

CAPS was awake, but his eyes were droopy and he looked like he might not make it through even a short conversation. He was propped up against his headboard by a mass of pillows and had been sipping some broth when Winston and I entered. He was wearing a tight muscle T-shirt (although on Caps there were no muscles per se to show off), and I could see several nasty bruises. He even had a large bandage wrapped around his head, making him look like one of those guys in old war movies who are recuperating in a field hospital in France and end up in love with the nurse.

He set his broth aside and glared when he saw me. "I don't want to talk with you. Go away."

His uncle went to his bedside and held up a placating hand. "I think you should listen to what he has to say."

"If he wants to apologize, he can forget it. Weasel can't talk his way out of this one."

I hoped he wasn't going to continue in this vein, as it was late and I wanted to have a nice, long, enjoyable romp with Tony before the sun came up. "You've got it all wrong, as usual, Caps."

"Oh?" he replied, letting the sarcasm drip.

"I was trying to give you a romantic boost as far as Sutton was concerned, but he seemed to think I was talking about myself rather than you, and he grabbed me and planted one on my lips. That's what you saw. I was trying to push him away."

"It didn't look like you were trying to push him away." Even as he said the words, though, Caps's eyes softened. He was beginning to see that he might have just walked in at the wrong moment, I could see. After all, I was his best bud. He surely knew I wouldn't do such a thing to him.

I went back over the scene I'd had with Sutton, filling in the details. As I spoke, Caps's granite stare crumbled, and he even managed a tiny smile.

"You fucked it up, you ass," he said when I'd finished.

"Well, I admit it could have gone better."

There was a short silence, which Caps eventually ended. "I'm sorry I attacked you."

"I'm sorry you hit your head on the wall."

"I hit it several times."

"I'm sorry you hit your head on the wall several times. So did I, by the way."

"You've got a thick skull, though."

I was trying to figure out if this was a burn when the uncle broke up our little dialog. "It's not the only thing he fucked up tonight," he told Caps, his tone not unkind. "Your friend here failed to get the safe combination."

"What? How on earth are you going to swap the wills now, you idiot?"

I rolled my eyes. "*You* were going to do the will swap, if you'll recall—"

"I can't now, not in the condition I'm in," Caps interrupted.

"—and it was your fault I didn't get it. You told me the wrong room. The room on the north side belongs to Kendrick."

"Did I say north?"

"You did."

"I meant south."

"Obviously."

"Sorry about that."

Winston waved his hands in the air. "The point is, gentlemen, that the wrong will is still in the safe, and when Freeman opens it, this Kendrick upstart will have all my money."

I sighed and looked at Winston kindly. "I don't see what we can do about it now. Freeman will undoubtedly be in bed by now. There's no way to get in and get the combination. Maybe we'll get a chance tomorrow."

Winston shook his head. "It may be too late then. I still think we should act tonight."

"How? If anyone goes into his room, he's sure to wake up."

"I had a long conversation with him earlier," the uncle said. "He told me he was a sound sleeper."

"He'd have to be nearly dead to sleep through someone coming in and going through his briefcase," I protested.

Winston pursed his lips. "He did have three glasses of wine with dinner."

"If it was bottles, you might get away with it."

"So you won't do it?"

I stared at the man. "Give me one good reason why I should! Look, I despise Tyler Kendrick as much as the next man, maybe more so. I still have the memories of the swirlies he gave me in middle school." Winston cocked a questioning eyebrow, so I elaborated. "A swirlie is where guy A, the bully, takes guy B, the victim, into the school restroom and shoves his head into one of the toilets. Guy A then flushes said toilet, causing the water to swirl. Thus, swirlie."

"Seems a pretty pointless activity."

"I always thought so."

"It makes no difference to you that he coaxed an older, sick lady into giving him most of her money in that damned will?"

"I hope he chokes on it, but nothing will sway me. There's no way I'm going into that lawyer's room while he's asleep in there. You can do it yourself."

"I can't! Believe me, I would if I could." Winston shrugged his shoulders. "But I've got a weak heart. It'd never hold up to the excitement."

"Then Caps can do it, if you really feel it has to be done."

Caps protested. "I can't stand right now without getting woozy!"

Winston gazed at his nephew with sad eyes. "I would think, Patrick, that you'd do this for your friend. After all, Jake would do this for me if he could."

"In a heartbeat," Caps agreed.

"But he can't," Winston said, shaking his head, "because of the damage you inflicted."

I sputtered. *"He* attacked *me.* His condition is his own doing."

Caps sniffed and gave me his best puppy-dog eyes. "I would think a good friend wouldn't hesitate. Remember, I get a Porsche out of this."

"And I'll get jail time! Look, I can't be caught searching yet another room! When Kendrick caught me, I managed to talk my way out of it, but that won't work here. I can hardly tell this lawyer dude that I've got a message for him from a woman that doesn't exist."

Winston's face brightened. "You can be one of the ghosts of Winston Hall. That way, in the case—and I stress that this won't happen—in the case that Freeman does awake, you'll be one of the spirits that roams the halls of this house. You just make some ghostly noise and slip out of the room. He'll be too shocked to think about following you."

"He'd never believe I was a ghost."

"He would!" I could see Winston was warming to his idea. His hands were gesturing wildly. "He was telling me earlier about his interest in the supernatural. He even said that he wouldn't mind running into one of the ghosts that haunt this place."

"There you go, Weasel," Caps said. "We just dress you up as Great-granddad Winston."

"He had half his face blown off, I thought you said. You may have noticed I've got a whole face."

"We can do it with makeup."

"Oh?" I laughed hollowly. "You've got a theatrical makeup kit handy?"

Caps's face darkened. "Ah. No. I hadn't thought of that."

"There's always," Winston said, "the Gray Lady."

"We can get you a gray dress out of Aunt Charlotte's closet," Caps added. "She's got plenty of wigs as well. And goodness knows you've had practice wearing women's clothes."

I eyed him coldly. If he thought he was helping his cause, he was sadly mistaken. "Plan all you want. I'm not going to do it."

Caps winced and put a hand to his head. He made sure I could see that the hand was shaky. "Keith told me that if I was still in pain in the morning that he'd have to drive me into town and have me checked out at the emergency room. I thought I wasn't too bad, but— did one of you guys just turn out the lights?"

I knew he was playing me, but I also knew when to throw in the towel. Caps really did look pretty pathetic lying there with his head bandaged. I sighed. "Give me an hour," I told them.

MY REASON for the hour delay before starting my life of crime was, of course, that I wanted to at least get in a little fun with Tony before donning Charlotte's wig and dress and doing the ghost thing. I needn't have bothered. When I traipsed down the hall to my own room, I quickly found that there was little reason for delay. I opened my door and was about to switch on the lights when I heard a soft snoring coming from the area of the bed. I quietly approached in the dark, and, sure enough, Tony was fast asleep. It occurred to me to wake him, but then I saw his sweet face in the moonlight as he snuggled against my pillow, and I couldn't bring myself to do it. With a disappointed heart, I returned to Caps's room. Sex in the morning with Tony would do just as well, I told myself. Provided I didn't end up in jail in the meantime.

Caps really was in bad shape. To give him credit, he did try to get out of bed to assist me in getting all ghosted up, but once he was on his feet, his knees decided that they really weren't up to the task, and he sank back into bed. He wished me luck, though, as Winston led me out of his room and we headed for the late Great-aunt Charlotte's lair.

It seemed that it had been some time since Mark Winston and Charlotte had shared a marital bed. His room, in fact, was clear down the hall, so I could see how easy it was for Charlotte to carry on an affair with Kendrick. They could have been yelling their heads off during the throes of ecstasy and he wouldn't have heard them.

Charlotte had made sure she had plenty of room, too. Not only was her bedroom bigger than my whole apartment, but she also had a walk-in closet you could have parked a fairly sizable car in. Winston quickly picked out a nice little dress and tossed it over to me.

"That should look spooky enough if seen in a dim light," he said, his face sour. "Mind you, it didn't do much for me in the stark light of day, either."

"I think we have a problem." I held the dress in front of me. "I'm six foot. I'm guessing your wife wasn't that tall. If I wear this, it'll look like a mini skirt."

"Ah. I hadn't thought of that." Winston fished around in the closet some more. "We'd better not go with a dress, then. Here's a blouse that should fit you. Luckily you're a skinny cuss."

"The word is trim."

"And… yes! I knew she had a long gray skirt. Won't be as long on you, of course."

"As long as nothing shows that shouldn't."

We grabbed extra garments, just in case, and headed back to Caps's room. Caps had his own bathroom, and I changed in there. I used a couple of Caps's socks to fill the bra. If seen, I didn't want the "ghost" to be flat-chested. That might arouse suspicion. The skirt covered my knees, so that was okay. I didn't bother with stockings. No one would get close enough to see the fine blond hair on my legs. Hell, hopefully no one would see me at all. I decided to forgo shoes entirely and do the roaming barefoot, just in case I had to bolt out of a room. I donned one of Charlotte's wigs and stepped out to let Winston and Caps critique the result.

If nothing else, I cheered Caps up. He tittered. "You look awful! A cross between Aunt Charlotte and Elton John!"

Winston, eager to keep me happy with the scheme, quickly shushed him. "You look fine," he said. "No one will see you anyway. Believe me, Freeman will sleep through the whole thing."

"I don't look much like a ghost, though," I said, looking down at my apparel uncertainly. "I just look like a lazy drag queen."

Winston gave this some thought, biting a nail as he racked his brain. Finally he smiled. "Be right back," he said. He headed out of the room but, true to his word, was back within a few minutes. He had a spray can in his hands.

"What's that?" I asked.

He showed me the label. "Leftover from last Christmas. It's flocking. You know, stuff you spray on the Christmas tree and windows to make it look all snowy. Close your eyes." With no further warning, he sprayed the stuff onto my face. He nodded at the result, then gave my arms and legs a good flocking. "I used it sparingly, so it should just kind of shimmer in the moonlight should anyone see you. That should give your appearance a ghostly glow."

Now my face and extremities felt sticky. "Or they'll think I'm a madman that someone sprayed with flocking."

"No one will see you anyway!"

"You should get going," Caps said. "It's getting late, and that will isn't going to swap itself." He leaned over and rummaged in the small drawer of his nightstand. He found a box of matches and tossed them to me.

"What are these for?"

Caps rolled his eyes. "So that you can see the combination, idiot! It'll be dark in there!"

"Good point." I sighed and stepped over to a mirror positioned over a small table. "Turn out the light," I told Winston. He did so and I examined my reflection. With the room barely lit by the meager moonlight coming in the window, I had to admit the flocking added a sort of otherworldly aspect. My face looked pale and had bits of sparkle to it. "I guess this will work. Hand over the will, if you'd be so kind, and I'll just get both tasks over with and be back here in fifteen minutes' time."

Caps and his uncle wished me luck as I strode to the door, gray skirt billowing about my legs.

Chapter Eleven

I DON'T know if you've ever entered someone's bedroom at two o'clock in the morning dressed as the ghost of a lady in gray with the intention of rifling through their briefcase. Probably not, I'm guessing. It's not something I recommend. My heart was thudding loudly in my chest as I padded down the hall on my tiptoes, and by the time I got to Freeman's door, it was pounding so loudly that Poe's telltale heart would have called it a show-off.

I paused at Freeman's door, my hand on the knob, to muster up the courage to actually turn the damned thing. I looked up and down the hall. Everything was quiet. There wasn't even any wind outside to rattle the window at the end of the hall. Slowly, I twisted the knob. It squeaked once but otherwise behaved itself. I pushed the door open.

There was enough light in the room, once my eyes had adjusted, to make out the bed and other furnishings, at least as big blobby things. On the bed was a huddled form. The form was snorting and mumbling occasionally. Freeman was indeed asleep. I crept over to the desk. On the top, sure enough, was a briefcase. Luckily it was already opened, so I didn't have to worry if it was locked. I shuffled through his collection of papers until I located a small notebook. I also snatched up one of his pens. I set these down in order to get to the box of matches I'd tucked into the waistband of Charlotte's skirt. Lighting a match, I quickly scanned the notebook.

It took three matches, but I finally found the safe combination. I used the pen and wrote it down on the back of my hand. The third match was beginning to burn out, so I dropped it and lit another. I had the combination but wanted to ensure it was legible.

The scratch of this match against the side of the box seemed to me to be louder than the others. I don't know if it really was significantly louder, but it did cause Freeman to let out a small cry, and he suddenly sat up in bed.

"What?" he called out, obviously disoriented. "What's going on? Who's that?"

I froze for a moment, not even daring to breathe. When he repeated his last question loudly enough to set off avalanches in Switzerland, I knew I couldn't just stand there like a statue, so I quickly blew out the match and turned to him.

"Oooooo-wooooooo," I moaned, trying to sound ghostly. I raised my arms and let them flutter a bit, hoping that added to the effect.

I could see his eyes grow wide. "Holy shit!" he exclaimed. His mouth fell open. "She really does exist!"

I made more "ooooo-woooo" sounds and surreptitiously dropped the pen onto the desk before beginning to make my way to the door. I was nearly there when he found the switch to a bedside lamp and turned it on. The room lit up and I let out a little yelp. Throwing open the door, I legged it out into the hall as behind me I heard the lawyer yelling out, "Hey!"

I slammed the door behind me. His shouting, though, had roused others. I could hear muffled voices coming from behind several closed doors. I pulled up my skirt and started running down the hall to Caps's room. I didn't get there, though. I'd only made a short dash before I heard the click of a knob. Someone a few doors down was in the act of coming out to the hall to see what the ruckus was about.

Panicking, I turned, thinking I could make the stairs and maybe hide somewhere downstairs. I realized I wouldn't make it, and, terrified, I just picked a door and threw myself inside, hoping against hope that it was an unoccupied room.

It wasn't. I could see the silhouette of a figure in bed. It was sitting up, grumbling and fumbling for the light. The search for a switch stopped when I came in. "What the hell?" the person growled as I closed the door behind me.

I recognized the growl as belonging to Tyler Kendrick.

The window in his room had no blinds, and he'd done a crappy job closing the curtains, so quite a lot of moonlight was filtering in. The bed area was mostly in shadows, but I'm sure I was at least faintly visible. Kendrick abandoned his search for the light and leaned forward in bed to get a better look at his intruder.

I raised my arms and emitted a weak "Ooo-woo." I figured it was worth a shot.

Kendrick scooted himself down to the bottom of the bed. I could now make out his features a little, and he was gaping at me in astonishment. I was just about to pull the wig off my head and say "I can explain" or something along those unlikely lines when he beat me to vocalizing by saying, "Kitty?"

I stopped my hand from plucking Charlotte's extra hair off my head just in time. "Um… yes," I said, remembering to use my Kitty voice.

"What in the world are you doing here? Hold on," he said, climbing out of the bed. "Let me get the lights."

I held up my hands. "No, don't do that. No lights. I don't want anyone to know I came into your room, and there seems to be a lot of commotion out in the hallway."

There was. I could hear my stepmonster angrily demanding why some damn fool had woken him up and Freeman loudly announcing that he'd seen a ghost. And while it was true that I didn't want the lights on, it was really because I knew that if he saw me clearly, Kendrick couldn't help but notice that it was just his hated rival in a wig and dress. Without Zach's amazing makeup job, I knew I couldn't pull off being Kitty.

Luckily Kendrick seemed to have forgotten about lights. "But," he asked, "what are you doing here?" He paused. "And why are you wearing glitter?"

Good question. What the hell would Kitty be doing at Winston Manor? "Um... I was chatting with my cousin earlier, and he mentioned that he was staying here for the weekend. And um... he mentioned that you were here as well, and... um...."

Kendrick walked toward me. In doing so, he strode across the beam of moonlight coming in through the window, and I could make out enough detail to see that his boxer shorts were tenting. And I'm not talking tenting just a little bit. I mean the presence of Kitty Wells in his bedroom at two thirty (or so, I only know it was late) in the morning was causing Kendrick to stick out like the Washington Monument among a bunch of bungalows. The boy was happy to see her. Unfortunately, I was her.

He came up and enveloped me in his arms. "And you sneaked into my room in the middle of the night? Oh, Kitty, you impetuous thing!" And he kissed me.

There are good kissers and bad kissers. Good kisser: Tony. Sweet, passionate, and his lips make every nerve in your body stand up and go, "Hey, what's this? What's going on, and can we make it go on longer?" And then there are your bad kissers. Case in point: Tyler Kendrick. My mouth thought it was being attacked by a squid. Big, freaky tongue forcing its way into my mouth like the villain in a Western movie coming through the saloon doors with a swagger. Too much saliva, and in all the wrong places. Honestly, during a kiss your cheeks should remain relatively dry. And then there was his moan, if that's what you want to call it. Under other circumstances, I'd have turned him around and given him the Heimlich maneuver, thinking he'd gotten a prawn lodged in his throat.

On the plus side, he squeezed me so hard that he popped my back. But again, you really shouldn't be hearing vertebra pop during a romantic moment.

But none of that compared to the sheer horror of feeling his erection pressing against my hip. Kendrick mistook my attempt to move back to get that evil thing off me as writhing in passion, I guess, because he increased his slobbering over my mouth and held me even tighter, which I wouldn't have thought possible.

I thought he was moving pretty fast, considering he'd exchanged maybe a few dozen words with Kitty and here he was poking his stiffness into her abs, but in fairness Kitty/me did show up suddenly in his bedroom in the middle of the night. I'd think she was a slut, too, if it happened to me.

"Oh, Kitty," he muttered, thankfully breaking off the oral attack long enough for that snake he called a tongue to form words. He took one of his massive paws and began fumbling around my chest, pushing and squeezing Great-aunt Charlotte's bra. "Oh, you're so firm," he groaned.

While I'm sure the Hanes company will be pleased to know that their socks make firm boobs, I doubt they'll be using this fact in their future advertisements. I had to get out of his clutches soon. Any second now the big oaf would be throwing me onto the bed and trying to stick his dick into Kitty's warm and waiting vagina, only to find that Kitty didn't have one and sported a fairly impressive pole instead. And how long before he got a look at my face in a moonlit area of the room?

His lips tried to swallow my mouth again, and my mind raced. I found myself wishing once again that the house really was just a big *Clue* game and I could bop him over the head with a lead pipe or a candlestick, but I saw no candlesticks handy and lead pipes were pretty scarce as well.

With no convenient weapons around, I did the only thing I could think of. I reached my hand down his shorts and found his stiff flesh. I'll give Kendrick this. It wasn't small. My hand briefly stroked his manhood, and then I reached down farther, finding his balls. I fondled them briefly and then squeezed. Hard. Really, really hard.

It had the desired effect. He immediately released me and, yelping like a kicked poodle, bent over, clutching his groin. The pain must have shot through his body, because his knees decided to give out, and he sank to the floor, hitting hard enough to cause a vibration throughout the room. Another strangled cry came out of his mouth and he found that being on his knees didn't allow for the writhing he wanted to do, so he fell over onto his back, holding himself and rolling back and forth.

"I'm sorry," I said, trying to sound coy. "Was that too rough?"

Tears were streaming down his face. "A bit," he squeaked.

"I'll get you some ice," I said, making for the door.

He may have said "Okay" or maybe it was just a whimper. I didn't linger or ask him to repeat himself. I was out the door in a flash.

In the hall, I had to lean against the wall for a moment to catch my breath. Being groped by Tyler Kendrick can take a lot out of a guy. I was so glad to be out of the room and away from his paws that at first I didn't even see the gaggle of people gathered at the other end of the hall. I vaguely heard murmuring and turned my head just as one of them, Freeman, spotted me.

"There it is! There's the ghost!" he shouted.

I couldn't tell you how many people were actually with Freeman or who they all were. I caught a glimpse of Cecily, dressed in a pink nightgown, and my stepmonster, dressed in ghastly striped pajamas, and a smattering of Winston relatives. That was all I took in before bolting for the stairs.

I did remember to make some "Ooo-wooo" noises as I went.

Chapter Twelve

I HOOFED it up to the attic, closing the door behind me just in time. I heard the posse rush down the hall and hit the stairs, but their steps receded as they made for the main floor. I collapsed against the door, happy I'd gone the right way. I could hear snatches of conversation as the ghost hunters went down the stairs. Apparently, I'd moved fast enough that most of the group either hadn't seen me or had seen me clearly enough to know what they'd seen. Cecily had seen "something," but she wasn't sure what it was. Dollings had been slow on the uptake and had "maybe" seen some shadow moving, but since according to him, ghosts were hokum, it had to be something else. Others were sure they'd caught sight of Winston Manor's Gray Lady.

Once I was sure the coast was clear, I pulled off the wig and trudged back down to Caps's room. He'd been dozing, but my footsteps woke him as I entered. As I flicked on the lights, he asked, "So how did it go?"

"On the plus side, I got the combination. On the minus side, half of the household is running around right now hunting for a ghost. Oh, yeah. And I was snogged by Tyler Kendrick."

Caps had been looking at me with that glazed I've-just-been-awakened look, but his eyes grew wide at the last revelation. "Really? How did that happen?"

I told him the whole tale. He was a good audience for most of it, nodding and shaking his head in commiseration at the appropriate places until I got to the Kendrick lip-lock. Here Caps chortled.

"Not funny, old friend. Even though the light was dim, I was almost crapping myself in fear that at any moment he'd see that it was me. He'd have killed me, and I didn't want the last person I kissed on this earth to be Kendrick."

"So how good a kisser is Kendrick?"

"It's like being mauled by a grizzly bear. You just yearn for sweet death."

Caps laughed some more. Once his hilarity had died, he said, "So you got the wills switched."

"I did not." I pulled the envelope out of my waistband. "Still have it here. I could hardly pop into the library and engage in illegal behavior with all those people roaming from room to room searching for the Gray Lady. No, I'll have to switch wills tomorrow night."

"You're cutting it rather close."

"Can't be helped. Now, if you'll excuse me, I need my clothes back so that I can get back to my room."

Still groggy from whatever Sutton had given him, Caps didn't protest. He was back to sleep before I pulled my jeans back on.

After washing off the flocking and leaving the Gray Lady garb in Caps's bathroom, I returned to my own digs. I quietly entered, not wanting to disturb Tony. I managed to strip off my clothes without rousing him, but he stirred as I slipped into bed.

"Where have you been?" he asked sleepily.

"That's a really long story. Tell you later." I kissed him on the cheek. "Sorry about leaving you like that."

"That's okay." Sleep hadn't entirely left him, and he was clumsy as he put his arms around me and pulled me close. We kissed briefly. "What time is it, anyway?"

"I don't know. Let's get a few hours' sleep and we can have a little fun in the morning."

Even though it was mere inches away, I couldn't make out much of his face. I was a better curtain closer than Kendrick was. Still, I could make out his smile. "Sounds good. What sort of fun did you have in mind?"

I rubbed my nose against his. "It's kind of like putting together toys on Christmas morning. You have to insert dowel rod A into slot B until it fits firmly…."

"Oh, yes?"

"…and then you move things around until you break something and make a big mess."

"Can't wait," he said sleepily.

TONY and I missed breakfast as we were still asleep, or at least I was. When my eyes eventually opened, he was leaning up in bed, propped by one elbow, watching me snooze.

"Good morning," he said.

It was. True, I was engaged to be married to a female biographer, my body ached from my spill down the stairs, I had Kendrick DNA on my lips, and I'd utterly failed to bring Sutton and Caps together, but I had Tony in bed with me.

I made the most of it.

I WOULD have gladly stayed in bed exploring the joy that was Tony until afternoon, but he had to serve luncheon to the weekend guests. Apparently breakfast was a serve-yourself affair, with Mrs. Donleavy putting the food out on the sideboard and everyone just digging in.

Lunch, at least in the Winston household, had to be served by a minion. I may have delayed Tony a little by continually kissing him as he attempted to dress.

He finally, with a grin, pushed my face away. "I've got to go. I'm late, and Mr. Winston likes lunch to be served on time."

I fought him a little, trying to push my kisser past his hands for another go. "Let Mrs. Donleavy serve the damn food."

"Are you crazy? She'd go ballistic! Come on, Weasel, you're going to get me fired."

After I reluctantly allowed Tony to depart, I got dressed myself. I figured I'd still be the most underdressed person at the table, but I did put on my best T-shirt, one emblazoned with the *Abbey Road* cover. Once attired, I traipsed downstairs to see what culinary delights Mrs. Donleavy had prepared for us.

In the dining room, there were a few scowls at my T-shirt. Obviously not everyone was a Beatles fan. My mood, after a fun morning romp with Tony, was too good to be dampened by a few old fogies who liked to dress up for their little tea parties. Ignoring their glares, I slid into my seat and made a show of placing my napkin on my lap. They were my good jeans, and I didn't want to slop soup onto them.

My good cheer suffered a slight blow when Cecily Talbot, wearing a red outfit and more makeup than a face should really support, sat next to me and gave my hand a little squeeze.

"Hello… fiancé!" she said with a giggle.

I scanned the faces around us and noted that no one seemed to have overheard. That was good. I didn't want to cause a lot of upset when I explained to Cecily that she had somehow mistaken something I'd said and that we weren't, contrary to her opinion, destined to walk down the aisle. Since she had only spilled the beans to the stepmonster so far, it wouldn't cause too much pain when I told her she was off her rocker. Nothing upsets a young gal like having to admit to friends and family that the guy she told them wants to marry her really has no such inclinations.

I frowned at her. "What exactly did I say to you when I woke up from my little tumble?"

She giggled again, this time coquettishly into her hand. "You mean when you proposed?"

"If you want to call it that."

"It was so romantic," she said with a sigh. "I asked you if you were all right, and you muttered something incomprehensible."

"I remember the incomprehensible part."

"And then I asked you if you wanted me to take care of you on a permanent basis—just as a joke, mind you—and you, very seriously, said that you'd like nothing better."

"Nothing better? Are you sure I didn't say something about melted butter? I think I wanted some toast. My words were a little fuzzy. Must have been hard to understand me."

"Oh, I heard you plainly when I asked you if you were asking me to marry you and you said yes."

I looked at her sadly. It wasn't really the little squeak's fault that she was in love with me. My dashing good looks have been both a blessing and a curse. Sometimes people hear what they want to hear. I remember one time after a particularly wild party waking up and asking the young man in bed with me to get off as his elbow was digging into my groin and he heard me inviting him to a hotel in Des Moines. To be fair, it had turned out to be a nice hotel.

"I need to tell you something, Cecily," I said.

"Yes, darling?"

The darling made me pause. I had to tread softly. It wouldn't do to have Talbot tears flowing into the soup with all the Winstons and assorted publishing bozos in attendance. "About what I said, I think—"

I was interrupted by my stepmonster, who took that moment to rise from his chair and tap his spoon against his water glass. Being a show-off, he was attired in an expensive suit with a perfectly tied tie. I didn't think he even owned a Beatles T-shirt, and he grew up in their era. Having gotten everyone's attention, he cleared his throat. "I have an announcement to make, and one, I must say, that gives me the greatest of pleasures."

"Um… better not," I said, sotto voce. I tried to waggle my eyebrows in warning, but the old goat didn't interpret the waggle correctly. He went on.

"I have the pleasure of not only welcoming a new author to the Dollings Press fold," he said, all smiles, "but also to the family. My stepson, Patrick, has asked Cecily Talbot to marry him, and she has accepted his request."

There were a lot of *Ah*s and *Well done*s from the table, and I believe a heard a rude crack about me getting some from Caps's grandfather at the end of the table. I sat there, dazed, unable to move or speak. I was just glad Tony wasn't in the room at the moment. I'm not sure how I could have explained my engagement to him. I couldn't even explain it to myself.

Papa Dollings asked me if I wanted to say a few words. I did, but I felt they weren't appropriate for the company so I waved the suggestion off. Cecily, though, stood up with a squeal.

"I'm just so happy," she gushed, "to be able to share this news with my friends and colleagues. You all mean so much to me, and Patrick and I wanted you to be the first to hear our wonderful news."

She moved to rumple my hair, but I was a little jumpy and I shifted my head just as her hand came at me, resulting in her fingers scrambling all over my face. One poked me in the eye, and I think one or two found their way into my nostrils. She laughed at this and leaned down to kiss my cheek. Everyone at the table applauded.

At that moment Tony entered with a cart and the main course was served. I think it was some sort of chicken. It was hard to tell as everything tasted of cardboard to me.

The meal passed by like a bad dream. People around me kept trying to engage me in conversation, but every time someone said something to me, I just looked at them and said, "Huh?"

At the end of the luncheon, Mark Winston announced that, according to a party tradition set by his late wife, there would be a croquet game and badminton out on the grounds for those who wanted to partake. Normally I'd have opted for the croquet, as I'm all for whacking wooden balls with mallets, but I was in no mood for games. Everyone headed for their rooms to change into less formal duds while I walked slowly toward the stairs. Tyler Kendrick stayed back as well, watching the throng disappear up the steps. When they were out of earshot, he took me by the elbow and pulled me aside.

"I thought I'd see your cousin at lunch today," he said with a frown. "She's here, I know, but I haven't seen her all morning. I thought about asking Mr. Winston where she was, but I haven't been able to get a word with him. She's not feeling ill, is she?"

"I don't believe so," I said weakly.

Kendrick sighed and nodded his head. "I know what it is. She accidentally hurt me last night. Just between you and me—" Here he gave me a knowing look, like we were old mates and always chatted about our conquests. "—she came to my room late last night. We started to get physical, if you know what I mean, and she got a little excited and, to be blunt, she gave my balls one hell of a twist. She's probably avoiding me out of embarrassment."

"Yeah," I said. "That's probably it."

"Is she around?"

If I hadn't suffered countless indignities at the man's hands, such as being stuffed in a locker during gym class on more than one occasion in high school, I might have felt sorry for the big galoot. As it was, I had other things to worry about. "She left," I said. "She drove back to Rockford early this morning."

He closed his eyes. "I was afraid of something like that. I'll give her a call. I've still got her number. I'll have to explain that while it hurt tremendously, I understand that it was just one of those accidents. I've been having trouble getting a signal out here, though. The Winstons must have a landline. Do you know where their phone is?"

"I wouldn't call her right away," I said. "She'll still be on the road."

"I thought you said she left early this morning. It's only a forty-five minute drive to Rockford."

"Um… yes. That's true." I was having trouble thinking. My head was full of visions of me in a monkey suit and Cecily Talbot all in white giggling as she walked up the aisle while the organ spewed out "The Wedding March." "She told me she was heading straight to bed once she got home, though. Didn't get much sleep last night, apparently."

Kendrick favored me with a wry smile. "That's true. It was late when she got to my room. Surprised the hell out of me, I have to admit, but it was a pleasant surprise." He stared at my face. "You know, I've never noticed before just how much of a family resemblance there is. You look a lot like her."

"We get that all the time."

He patted my shoulder and left me, saying he wanted to get in on the badminton game. I decided I'd wander around the grounds to try to clear my head. It was a little chilly, so I grabbed my hoodie before heading out. Leaving my room, I nearly did another tumble down the stairs when I came across young Ernie down on all fours at the top of the steps. After I nearly fell over him, he stood up with a guilty look on his face.

"Hello," he said.

I arched an eyebrow. "What are you up to?"

"Nothing. Absolutely nothing."

You can't bullshit a bullshitter. I knew he was lying. I cranked up the eyebrow another notch, letting him know I wasn't going to let his answer stand.

His shoulders sank. "I'm looking for Jeffrey."

"The tarantula?"

Ernie frowned. "How many Jeffreys do you know that I'd be looking for? Of course the tarantula!"

"He got out?"

The kid gave me one of those you-are-too-stupid-to-live looks. "Yeah. That's kind of why I'm looking for him. I was playing with him, and he got away from me."

I couldn't find myself blaming the spider much. If I was a tarantula forced to play with a snot-nosed kid like Ernie, I'd probably make for the hills myself. Still, the youngster looked fairly sad over his loss, so I said, "Well, I'm sure he'll show up sooner or later."

The kid looked less than reassured. "I've looked everywhere for him. I think he's lost for good."

"Well, I'll certainly keep an eye peeled for him." I spoke the truth. It would be disconcerting, to say the least, to crawl into bed for the evening only to find that the bed was already occupied by a tarantula.

"Don't tell my mom that I've lost him," the kid said, his face forlorn. "She'll only yell at me."

"Jeffrey will be back in his cage before she finds out about his being AWOL, I'm sure. He's probably just stretching his numerous legs. Once he's bored with that, he'll come crawling back to you, tail tucked between two of his legs."

"Spiders don't have tails."

"It's just an expression, you chump."

"It's a dumb one to apply to spiders."

Suddenly I wished I'd fallen over the kid and tumbled once again down the stairs. I'd at least be closer to the door. I maneuvered my long legs around the boy and continued on. "Be that as it may," I said over my shoulder, "I need some fresh air. Good luck with the spider hunt!"

The kid muttered something which I'm sure was meant to be offensive. I ignored him and moved at a brisk pace until I was down the stairs and out the front door.

Once out in the cool air, I walked slowly, my head bowed in thought. I rambled. There were trees and grass and rocks and some bushes and I think maybe a brook somewhere at the rear of the property, but I noticed little of it. I kept rehearsing conversations in my head in which I gently told Cecily she was mad as a hatter if she thought we were getting hitched. All of them would no doubt end with me getting my face slapped, but that was a small price to pay.

I was so engrossed in thought that I nearly walked right into the middle of the croquet game. Although I hadn't realized it, I'd circled the house and had come upon the playing ground. Caps, who was feeling well enough not only to play but had removed the stupid-looking bandage from around his head, shouted a warning to me, stopping me before I strolled into the path of a shot that my stepmonster had just made. His wooden ball with a red stripe narrowly missed the tip of my Nikes.

"Care to join us?" Dollings asked. He was scarily friendly now that he believed I was engaged. I think I liked him better when he despised me.

I moved to the sidelines, my hands stuffed into my pockets. "I'm fine," I said.

Off to the right, two badminton nets had been set up, and teams had formed. The croquet was less popular, with only Pops Dollings, Caps, Cecily, Freeman, and the dreaded Aunt Ericka playing. Idly, I looked around for Tony, but as a paid servant he must not have been invited to the festivities. The cook, Mrs. Donleavy was also notable for her absence.

It occurred to me that with nearly everyone out and enjoying the day, chilly and overcast as it was, that it might be a good time to pop inside and do the will swap. I was about to stroll toward the house when a voice came from right behind me.

"You and I seem to be the only two not playing."

I turned to see Keith Sutton standing there. The nurse had a box of gumdrops in his hand. He fished one out, tossed it up in the air, and deftly caught the sweet in his mouth.

"Seems that way," I said.

"Odd you getting engaged," he said, catching another gumdrop in midair.

"Very odd," I agreed.

"You see," he continued, a black gumdrop bouncing off his nose and plummeting to the ground, "I kind of thought you had a thing for me." He glared at the fallen gumdrop as if it had committed a heinous crime.

I shook my head. "You got the signals all wrong yesterday, I'm afraid."

"Seems I did. I had no idea you were straight. You don't look straight. Plus, you did tell me you were gay."

I bristled at the you-don't-look-straight remark but decided to let it pass. I looked over to see Caps glaring in our direction. While I had explained the situation to my friend, he still appeared to dislike seeing me in close conversation with the nurse. I spotted an area not too far off with some bushes and a hedge where I could talk to Sutton without us being overheard. "Let's go over here and I'll try to explain things," I said.

We strode over, but he stopped as we got on the other side of the hedge to pop another gumdrop into his mouth. "What was all that guff about finding the right guy if you weren't coming on to me? Or was I just going to be a last fling before you got married?"

I shook my head. "You have it all wrong, friend. I was trying to tell you that someone, not me, was infatuated with you."

He eyed me suspiciously. "You mean your buddy, Jake."

I smiled. "Exactly. Jake. A really nice guy, and a good catch for anyone."

"He's got stringy hair."

"The gene pool did desert Caps in the hair department, but once you get used to it, it's not bad. Besides, I've seen Caps with short hair, and believe me, you don't want that. Frightens dogs and small children."

"And he's got no chin."

"Saves a lot of money on shaving cream, I expect. Chins aren't everything. You must look beyond these superficial features, Sutton, and see the true Caps. He's a great guy."

Sutton smiled and shook his head. The hand not holding the gumdrop box snaked out and grabbed hold of my wrist. He went so far as to give it a little rub. "I usually date hot guys. You're a bit on the skinny side for me, but you're good-looking."

I managed to free my hand by pretending to have to scratch my nose. "And what does dating good-looking guys get you? We can't be trusted. Look at me! I'm engaged to Cecily over there." I pointed across the hedge. "Guys like me are nothing but trouble. You need someone cute but simple, like Caps."

"He's not cute."

"You're not squinting enough. Seriously, though. I thought he was a bit homely when I first met him, too. Then I got to know him, and I thought he was remarkably cute. I'd have dated him myself, but we were already friends by then. That and we were fourteen at the time."

Sutton moved in closer to me, giving me the full force of his twinkling eyes and smile. "I'd much prefer having some fun with you."

I found myself not liking this Sutton. I didn't think he was good enough for Caps. Not only was he superficial, but he wouldn't take no for an answer. Plus, I'm pretty sure he was a slut. He seemed to think that all he had to do was bat his eyelashes at me and I'd be panting and dropping my trousers at the earliest convenience. I stepped back from him.

"Sorry, my friend. I'm taken."

Technically I was, by Cecily, but I had hopes to end that "taken" and add a "taken" in conjunction with Tony. Sutton shrugged and removed another gumdrop from the box.

"Your loss," he said as he tossed it into the air. He moved his mouth under the drop's trajectory and neatly caught it.

"I'll live," I replied.

"Gackkkkk," he said.

I looked at him, wondering if I'd heard correctly. It took me a moment to realize that the gumdrop had lodged in his throat and Sutton was having difficulty breathing. In seconds his face turned red and he had panic in his eyes.

"Jesus!" I yelled. I wasn't fond of the guy, but I didn't want him to choke to death. "Can you breathe?"

He made some motions with his hands, telling me he could not. I quickly moved behind him and put my arms around his chest, getting my hands double-fisted just under his sternum. You'd think a nurse would have realized I was doing the Heimlich maneuver, but maybe he was panicking. He tried to break free of me. Being stronger than I look, I jerked him back. We did this to and fro thing for several seconds until it dawned on him that I was attempting to save his life, and he allowed me to Heimlich him. It took four squeeze-thrusts against his abdomen before the offending gumdrop flew out of his mouth.

Sutton gasped in air, the hedge helping to hold him up. Panting heavily with tears running down his cheeks, he managed to gasp out, "Thanks!"

"Least I could do," I said. "I could have done that much faster, mind you, if you hadn't fought me. I know you were panicking and all, but I would have thought...."

I let the sentence trail off. As I was speaking, I looked back over to the croquet game. While the other players were concentrating on their balls and what shots they were going to take next, Caps was staring our way, hatred in his eyes. The hatred, I knew, was directed at me.

I was confused at first before I realized what Caps must have seen. Me, behind Sutton, pulling him against me several times before making some thrusting motions. With the hedge between me and the croquet game, Caps could only see the above-the-waist action. I can only imagine what he thought was going on below the waist.

I wouldn't have thought anyone could mistake the Heimlich maneuver for a bit of rump pounding, but that was obviously what put the look of murder in Caps's eyes. He stood, fuming, with his shoulders heaving. Then he let out a war cry—strikingly similar to the one he shouted before we both went down the stairs the difficult way—and, brandishing his croquet mallet like a club, ran toward us.

I gulped. Then I turned and ran.

Again, I must point out that under normal circumstances, I wouldn't be worried about Caps. While we both resemble figures made out of pipe cleaners, my pipe cleaner figure has the stronger muscle tone. Plus, I'm not a bad fighter, having had a lot of experience tussling with hoodlums at my high school who thought "the faggot" would be easy pickings. However, a Caps wielding a croquet mallet and swinging it madly while screaming at the top of his lungs should be avoided. Therefore I hoofed it, leaving a panting Sutton holding on to a hedge for dear life.

It might have looked comic to someone looking on from afar, me running across the Winston lawns pursued by a seeming madman with a mallet, both of us shouting. My shouts were along the lines of "But I can explain!" while his were more of the "I'm going to kill you, you fucking bastard!" variety. Being the one threatened with the mallet, I couldn't pause to see the humorous side of the situation. I was too busy running.

I'm more the sprinter type. Caps had done some cross-country running for the school, so I knew he'd outlast me in the long run. I saw a big oak tree in the distance and made for that, the idea being that I could run around, keeping tree between me and mallet, until I could get Caps to stop acting like a fathead and listen. I just needed to point out to him the fact that if I had been playing hide the salami with Sutton, we had performed quite a magic trick as both our pants were up and secured around our hips, zippers in the upright position. Hard to fuck without the genitals actually out and waving free.

I made it to the tree and circled it, but Caps was giving me no chance to explain. He swung the mallet, hitting the tree. The head of the mallet broke off, leaving Caps with a makeshift spear. "I'm going to kill you, Weasel!" he screamed.

"It's not what you think!" I shouted back, ducking and moving as he swung again. I ran to the other side of the tree. "Use your head, Caps! Would we be fucking where everyone could see us?"

"You've done it before!" Another swing as he came up behind me. I felt the tip of his broken mallet nick my hood as I scampered away. "What about you and Brandon Price?"

The incident he was referring to had happened several years previously. Brandon had been an aspiring actor, and we'd had a hot and heavy affair for a week or so. One afternoon, during a break while he was rehearsing, we thought we'd hide behind the curtain on the stage and do it. How were we to know some idiot would choose the wrong moment to test opening the curtain? "That was different!"

"Face it, Weasel! You'll fuck anything, anytime, anywhere!" Caps had decided that the usefulness of the mallet as a club, now that the head was shattered, had pretty much run its course, so he tried jabbing me with it. He was fast, but I was faster. I'll give Caps his due. If we were in a race, my money would be on him. But there's something about a having a crazed lunatic trying to poke you with the sharp end of a broken croquet mallet that gives you some extra oomph. Unfortunately, going around and around the damned tree was getting me dizzy. I darted off toward the rear of the Winston property.

"Come back here, you coward!" Caps called as he took off after me.

"Why? So you can stab me?"

"Yes!"

I would have pointed out that, from my point of view, this was hardly an advantageous option. It might have made Caps feel better, but it would result in serious damage to the Weasley internal organs, and I'm very fond of them. I decided, though, to keep these observations to myself. I needed to save my breath and energy for the running.

And run I did. We ran out of Winston land and hit a wooded area. I allowed myself a quick backward glance to see that Caps was close on my heels, jabbing away with his damned mallet. I called on my inner reserves and went faster.

We crashed through the woods, probably disturbing several woodland creatures who were enjoying a midafternoon snack. In passing, I noticed a squirrel on a branch of a tree that seemed to be eying us and branding us idiots before resuming his grooming ritual. My cell phone chose this moment to ring in my pocket, but I felt this was no time for idle chatter.

It's not easy to run fast through woods. There are branches and rocks and all sorts of things to trip you up, but somehow I managed to avoid all obstacles. Caps wasn't so lucky. I easily leaped over a log lying across the path we were running along. Seconds after that, I heard a crash. I dared a look back. Caps, cursing, was getting back to his feet after tumbling over the log. This seemed to anger him even more, although it seemed to me he should have wanted to take his frustrations out on the log rather than me. However, he emitted another war cry and resumed the chase.

The woods ended, and while I was thankful I no longer had to avoid trees and rocks, I had a new problem. Some damned fool had decided to put a small lake beyond the woods. I quickly scanned the area. Sure, I could run left or right and go around the lake, but that looked really far, and I knew I'd run out of steam before long. Before me was a rickety wooden pier leading out over the water. I ran to the pier. I think I was hoping there would be a small boat or canoe tied to one of the posts, but there wasn't. Halfway across the pier, I realized I had two options: leaping into the water when I ran out of pier or turning and facing Caps. I got to the end of the pier and turned, not wanting to take a dip into the cold October waters.

A wild look came over Caps's eyes as he saw that he had me. He held up his spear, and, screaming something about blood, death, and destruction, ran the last few yards toward me.

"Now, Caps," I said, my tone reasonable if somewhat breathy after our run. Seeing he wouldn't listen to words and not wanting to get poked with his spear, I ducked, trying to make myself as small a target as possible.

Caps hit me, but he hadn't compensated for a Weasley in ducked mode. He tripped over me and then flipped and hit the water, making one hell of a splash. Enough water slopped over me to tell me that my assessment of the water temperature had been correct. It was pretty cold.

I waited long enough to see Caps come up for air, spitting water. Seeing he was okay, I took off back down the pier.

Chapter Thirteen

DINNER that night in Winston Manor was a somber affair, for me at least. Cecily seemed quite chipper, grabbing my hand whenever she wasn't engaged in scooping fish into her mouth. The stepmonster, having heard of my cross-country jaunt that resulted in Jake Winston taking an unexpected swim, glared at me in warning, as if to say, "I was starting to be proud of you—don't louse this up!" Sutton often gave me dark looks as well. He had found a soaking wet and muttering Caps wandering back to the house and had helped him inside, forcing him into bed with some hot broth. His looks were asking, "Why are you trying to kill your friend?" Kendrick was way down the table from me, but he, too, found time to shoot me a frown. The furrowed brow of young Ernie was not directed at me, as his worry was over the loss of his spider. His mother, the dreaded Aunt Ericka, also frequently shot me looks meant to kill, but I think that was simply routine with her.

I knew the reason for Kendrick's frown. After getting back to the house, chilled and frankly tired out, I checked my phone to see what idiot had been calling me while I'd been in a life or death struggle with a mallet-wielding idiot. My blood froze when I saw that it had been Kendrick calling, trying to reach Kitty. When I didn't answer, Kendrick's call had gone to my voice mail, and now Kendrick no doubt wanted to know why my voice was on Kitty's mailbox. I hoped by dessert I'd have an answer for that.

To take his mind off his missing spider, Ernie had turned to the world of art. During the afternoon he'd attacked a watercolor set he'd found, as evidenced by splotches of color still on his hands and even his face. The resulting masterpiece was passed to me for inspection. It was a portrait of Jeffrey.

"Not bad," I said truthfully as I passed it back to him, going behind his mother's back to do so. I'm not up on spider paintings, but this one seemed to do the subject justice. The kid at least had the right number of legs on the arachnid, all of which were appropriately hairy. Ernie thanked me for the critique, and we returned to the grub before us.

The only good thing about dinner was that I got to give Tony flirtatious looks every time he came around to scoop peas onto my plate or refill my wine glass. I thought I was being discreet with these looks, but Cecily caught one of them and gave my hand a particularly hard squeeze.

"Should we discuss dates?" she asked.

I thought it was pretty late to think about going out on dates now that we were engaged, but any woman soppy enough to believe she was engaged to a gay guy she had never even kissed on the lips could be capable of nearly anything. "Um… how about dinner and a movie?" I asked.

She tittered. "Not that kind of date, silly! A date for the wedding!"

Tony, in the process of topping up my glass, let the wine overflow. A red stain quickly spread, which he and I both did our best to mop up with napkins. "I'm so sorry, sir," he said, his tone not the friendliest. Nor was the glance he spared me before he retreated back to the kitchen. It seemed everyone had a hateful glare for old Weasel. If the Winstons had a family dog, the mutt would undoubtedly sniff and roll his eyes in my direction, thinking the kibble he hadn't enjoyed was somehow my fault.

The wedding nonsense had to stop, no matter how much it would infuriate my stepmonster. "Let's discuss this after dinner," I told Cecily, still sopping up wine. As I munched on my fish, I rehearsed more speeches in my head, breaking it off with the deluded writer. I found it hard, however, to write speeches in my head with everyone glowering at me.

After dinner it was my intention to first head up to Caps's room, where Sutton had insisted my friend remain to rest after his dunk in the lake. I'd explain the situation to him and then head back downstairs to break off the engagement. My plans were foiled, though, when, after the throng had wolfed down the last of the food and people were milling through the door, I was stopped by an angry-looking Kendrick.

"You've got some explaining to do," he said, making sure the bulk of his body was between me and the door.

"Do I?" I tried the haughty approach. "Let me pass, Kendrick. I don't have time to talk right now."

He slapped a hand onto my shoulder, fixing me in place. "You're not going anywhere until you tell me what's going on with your cousin. I tried to call her earlier and got you on voice mail. What gives?"

I cocked an eyebrow at him. "Well, it's obvious, isn't it?"

"Is it? I think there's something fishy going on with you and her, and I want to know what it is."

I barked out a laugh. "At a guess, I'd say that when she forked over her phone number to you, she had the sense not to give out her own. She gave you my number. Surely you don't think a nice girl like Kitty would just give out her number to anyone who asked?"

I hoped he wouldn't think through how nice she must be if she also drove for miles to show up in bedrooms in the middle of the night. He didn't. He nodded at my explanation. I felt like nodding myself. I certainly nodded at dinner when the answer came to me. It was so simple but took me forever to come up with it. My mind had been too filled with wills, angry friends coming at me with spears, and being engaged to be bothered with easy solutions. That's my excuse and I'm sticking to it.

"Could you," he asked, his body language relaxing a little, "give her a message for me?"

"Certainly." She would, in fact, hear the message at the same time as me.

"Tell her to call me. Tell her I'm not angry or upset. I know she just got carried away. Would you do that for me?"

I assured him I would. Kendrick was a pretty forgiving sort, at least where women were concerned. If someone had twisted my balls the way I'd twisted his, they'd be off my Christmas card list for life.

Satisfied, Kendrick removed his bulk from the door and allowed me to pass. I thought I was free to traipse up the stairs to Caps's room, but I was wrong. At the bottom of the stairs, a very stern Jasper K. Dollings was waiting for me. His frown was so deep that families of moles could have made their homes in the furrows.

"So there you are," he said. "I've been waiting to have a word with you."

"Oh?"

"I heard about your little escapade with that friend of yours this afternoon. Running all over the place like idiots."

"A little misunderstanding."

"I heard you threw him in the lake."

"Not true. He sort of barreled over me and flipped into it. His own fault entirely."

The stepmonster sighed heavily and fixed me with the evil eye. "I thought you were going to grow up and dispense with these childish shenanigans."

"Wasn't my idea. Caps chased me with a croquet mallet."

"So? You thought this was an excuse to run around like a fool?"

"I object to being hit with croquet mallets."

Dollings grabbed the front of my T-shirt and pulled me closer. His lip was curled. "Look, you little shit. If mess up your engagement to Cecily Talbot, I'll hurt you. I don't know how, but I will. I'll see that that car of yours is taken away from you, for one."

"But that's my car!"

"It's in your mother's name."

That was true, and he might even convince my mother to take it away from me. I figured I'd try to appeal to his better nature. I wasn't sure he had one, but I thought I'd try. "Doesn't it strike you as odd that this girl wants to get hitched to me and she's never even dated me? We've never even kissed!"

"Probably why she agreed. She doesn't know what an imbecile you are. I recommend a quick wedding, before she realizes what a fathead you are."

"You don't find her odd?"

There was a slight flicker of doubt in his eye. "She's... eccentric, of course. A lot of writers are. But she's obviously smitten with you, so go with it." He released my T-shirt.

I wasn't going to give up on finding this man's better nature. "Now that I've spent some time with her, I'm beginning to think she might not be all there." Actually, I knew this after knowing her five minutes.

"She wants to marry you; it goes without saying that she's not all there."

Okay, no better nature. Let's try for appealing to his religious convictions. "Maybe I was too hasty in proposing." Maybe I did it while delirious. "I mean, we barely know each other. Haven't even talked that much. Wouldn't it be best to break it off and wait? I don't want to destroy the sanctity of marriage, after all."

It was the wrong thing to say. During the first part of my little speech, he seemed to be softening, a paternal twinkle even showing in his eye. I could see he was just brimming with stepfatherly advice to dole out. However, the mention of the sanctity of marriage made him square his shoulders, and back came the lip curl. "Listen, you little worm," he growled. "The reason most marriages don't work out is because young varmints like you don't wait for the honeymoon bed to have sex with their partners. Promiscuity and homosexuality are the main dangers to marriage. The first part of marriage should be getting to know your partner." Having snarled this out, he put a hand on my shoulder and attempted a smile. "No, you're following the correct course. Cecily obviously loves you. That's all that matters."

I thought that the fact I wanted to sleep with boys, particularly Tony, might enter into the equation, but I thought I'd keep this tidbit to myself. I'd seen that snarl of Dollings's in loads of horror movies, just before the snarler sprouted hair and a snout and began howling at the moon and ripping anyone fool enough to be nearby completely to shreds.

Dollings wasn't finished. "Don't mess this up. Frolicking around with your buddy might lead Cecily to think you're not mature enough for marriage."

"Maybe I'm not."

You know that look Lon Chaney as the Wolf Man gave as he was about to eat Evelyn Ankers? That was the look I got. "You'd better be," Dollings said. A little bit of spittle collected on his bottom lip. "I've prayed for you until I've run out of prayers. This is the first thing you've done that has made me not be embarrassed to be your stepfather." He took in air. I think he counted to ten. Then he patted my shoulder again. "You're just having jitters from realizing you're growing up. That happens. The best of us have second thoughts after asking a woman to marry us. I even wondered if asking your mother to marry me was the right thing to do after meeting you. You'll be fine."

I wouldn't, but he didn't care to hear that, so I just nodded. He finally left me to my thoughts. I'd have to put off for now telling the loon that the marriage was off, but I still had to chat with Tony and Caps and put things right with them. I decided to head to Caps's room first.

He threw a pillow at me when I entered the room. I ducked and it hit the door behind me. Immediately I held up my hands in supplication. "If you'll just listen to me, I—"

I stopped because he was laughing. The chortling went on, it seemed to me, a little too long, and at one point he pointed a finger at me and went into even deeper spasms of hysteria, his face red. A few tears even dripped down his cheeks. I was glad he was enjoying himself, but I was growing tired of waiting to find out what the joke was, especially as it seemed to be directed at yours truly.

Finally Caps coughed a few times and cleared his throat. "I'm not mad," he said. Another laughing jag hit him, and I had to wait another full minute.

"I gathered that," I said.

"Keith told me what happened. He said you saved his life."

"Anyone who eats gumdrops that way is asking for trouble. What I can't understand, even bearing in mind that your mind is subpar, how you mistook the Heimlich maneuver for having sex."

"I could only see you from the waist up. How did I know you didn't have your pants down? And you were behind him, pulling at his hips."

"He was being squirrelly, trying to get away. I had to keep pulling him back."

"Well, then, you can see why I thought what I did."

"No, I can't. In full view of everyone playing croquet? In front of my stepmonster?"

Caps shrugged. "I figured you were in the throes of passion and didn't notice the people across the lawn. I guess I wasn't thinking."

"You've been doing a lot of not thinking lately."

"Well, after John Adair—"

"You really need to let that go."

He smiled to show the subject was closed. "So, what time are we swapping wills tonight?"

"We? You've decided to join me?"

"I figured it was the least I could do to show there were no hard feelings. One of us can keep watch while the other opens the safe."

I knew who would be the one doing the actual safe opening, but I simply nodded. Having Caps there to watch the hall to make sure no one popped in would makes things much easier and would make me feel a lot better. "Let's go for two in the morning. Everyone should be in bed and asleep by then." Now that we were chummy again, I sat on the edge of his bed. "I don't think we should plan on earlier. After last night, it's obvious this group is up and roaming the halls fairly late."

We chatted for a while longer, going over some of the details of Operation Will Swap. We decided that since we wouldn't be going into anyone's bedrooms, dressing up as famous Winston Manor ghosts wouldn't be necessary. We'd just wear dark clothing.

"I've got some black ski masks we could wear," Caps offered.

"Won't that make us look like criminals?"

"Well, since you keep on harping on about this being illegal anyway, they might be appropriate."

I conceded the point. We agreed to meet in his room at the stroke of two.

Chapter Fourteen

IT WAS with a lighter heart, therefore, that I headed downstairs to the kitchen. True, I was still engaged to some lunatic woman, but Caps and I were friends once again and things were looking up. If I could get back on track with Tony, a feat which I knew I could accomplish with a few short paragraphs and earnest looks, everything would be hunky if not dory.

In the kitchen I found Mrs. Donleavy toiling away, washing the dishes. Tony was assisting her. When he saw me, the smile vanished from his lips and he refused to acknowledge my presence. The good Mrs. Donleavy, sensing the tension in the air, found an excuse to leave the room.

"I'd better check the larder and make sure there's enough for tomorrow's lunch," she said, shutting off her rinse water. With a knowing look for both Tony and me, she departed.

I hovered near the doorway, feeling uncomfortable. Tony turned away, busying himself with putting away some of the washed and dried dinnerware.

"Hello," I said as an icebreaker.

Tony grunted something in return. I couldn't catch all of it, but "get stuffed" was certainly part of the sentence.

"There might be a storm tonight. The sky is looking a little angry outside."

Another grunt.

"Could be worse, I suppose. If it were much colder, we could get snow."

"That," he said without turning, "would be awful. Tell me, does your fiancée know you're down here, visiting with the hired help?"

"I can explain about that."

Tony turned and glared at me. "I can hardly wait to hear this one."

I began to regale him with my tale. I told it well, if I do say so myself. I went for the light tone, painting myself as the hapless victim of the story, with the stepmonster and Cecily taking the roles of the evil villain and deluded damsel respectively. A quarter of the way through my tale I saw the corners of Tony's mouth curl slightly. Halfway through he was smiling outright and shaking his head in amused sympathy. When I got to the socko ending, he laughed and motioned for me to come over for a hug. We engaged in some kissing as well.

"You're an idiot," he said before planting another wet one on my lips.

"It's been mentioned before," I agreed.

More conversation was put on hold while we kissed and did some minor groping. We parted, both of us blushing a little, when Mrs. Donleavy returned some minutes later. Her lips were tight when she spotted two young men engaged in some tongue wrestling in her kitchen, but her eyes were twinkling.

"Don't mind me," she said. "Believe me, I've seen worse in my day. Besides, two boys kissing is hot." And here she wiggled her eyebrows and smiled.

Still flushed and unable to meet anyone's eyes, Tony returned to the sink and quickly began to dry more dishes. To change the subject, he said, "Speaking of seeing things, did either of you see Jake Winston when he came back to the house this afternoon? He was soaking wet."

I held up my hand like the guilty child in a kindergarten classroom. "That was me as well," I said. I told them the story, this time really playing up the humor. I used one of the kitchen chairs, pretending it was a choking Keith Sutton and exaggerated pulling it back against me repeatedly, giving the impression that the act had looked more lascivious than it really had, except in Caps's eyes. Mr. Donleavy laughed heartily and every now and then exclaimed a "My goodness" or an "Oh, you naughty boy, you." Tony chuckled a lot and often shook his head, which I took as a good sign. His demeanor was that of a guy who was falling for the storyteller, even though part of him was—probably rightly so—telling him this guy may be more trouble than he's worth. When I finished, Mrs. Donleavy insisted we open up a bottle of wine. We sat around the table and drank a bit until she suggested the two of us open another bottle and go off somewhere, leaving her to finish her work in peace.

When we got to the stairs, I suggested we go to his room. I couldn't shake the image of us all naked and midcoitus and my stepmonster bursting in. Sadly, he shook his head.

"I share my room with Andrew."

"Who's Andrew?"

"He's the other guy they hired to help out this weekend."

This came as news to me, as I was only aware of him and Mrs. Donleavy. I said as much.

"Andrew's a bit slow, mentally. He's mostly helped Mrs. Donleavy with breakfasts so far, helping to carry the dishes and stuff to the dining room. He's been pretty sick though, and has been in bed for most of the time. That nurse, Sutton, looks in on him every now and then. I guess it's a touch of the flu or something."

Armed with our wine, I wanted to find a quiet place to continue to get to know Tony, but I still was wary of going to my room. "I wish there was somewhere we could go that was further away from the throng than my room. You know, just in case we get carried away and you scream in ecstasy."

"It might be you doing the yelling!" he said, playfully punching my arm. He led the way up the stairs. "Follow me. I know just the place we can go."

We left behind us the sounds of mirth coming from the card room, where undoubtedly another rousing game of bridge was in progress. I figured Tony was taking me to some uninhabited bedroom, but instead he led me down the hall to a winding staircase, which I assumed led up to the tower room I had spotted when Caps and I had first arrived. This turned out to be the case, as we ended up in a rounded room which had, in its day, been used as a nursery. There were several old-fashioned school desks in the center of the room, complete with a storage compartment where the student could store pens, books, and a spider to scare the governess with during the daily lessons. The desks were pretty old, evidenced by not only the condition but the fact that they had a place to put your bottle of ink. There were also some toys littered about the room, such as a rocking horse and several dolls, most of them decapitated. Off to the side was a small bed, no doubt there so that the little nippers could nap, if need be. While the room hadn't been used in ages, someone had cleaned it every now and then, since there wasn't an inch of dust covering every surface. Ernie obviously had played here. One desk bore the remnants of his artistic endeavors and the spider portrait had been pinned up on one wall.

Tony set the wine bottle and our two glasses down on one of the desks before drawing me close to him for a kiss. "Far enough away from the crowd for your liking?"

"This will do," I replied. "I note you found a room with a bed. You little rascal, you."

"I thought we might need to sit on it. The desks are too small for us."

"That's true."

"And after your escapades this afternoon, I thought you might be a little tired."

I gave him a long, lingering kiss. "Strangely, I don't feel a bit tired. How about you? Has serving all that food worn you out?"

He grinned. "I think I've got some energy left."

We opened the wine and drank some before going over to sit on the edge of the bed. It wasn't the most comfortable mattress, but it would do. Besides, I could put up with a bed of nails if Tony was the reward. We sat there for quite a while, talking and occasionally kissing. I learned a lot about him, such as he'd been a wrestler in high school, he'd thought about becoming a forest ranger, and he didn't like broccoli or fish. I told him some more about myself and some of my exploits. When I told him about being arrested for swimming nude in the fountain at Purdue University, he chuckled and eyed me suspiciously.

"I'm never sure if you're telling me the truth or not," he said, snuggling closer. "But then, anyone who can get themselves engaged to a woman they barely know is capable of nearly anything." He leaned his head on my shoulder. "You're trouble, aren't you, Weasel?"

"I don't try to be."

"I think that's part of the problem. You're one of those guys that lives in the moment. You never think about consequences. You just blunder into a situation. Damn the torpedoes! Full steam ahead!" He sighed. "It'd be terrifying dating you."

"Would you like to find out?"

He shifted his head, getting comfortable. "You live in Rockford, right? Pretty far away."

"There's this thing called the automobile. Makes long distances less long. We're only an hour or so drive away from each other. And my ride's a Corvette. Eats up those miles fairly quickly." That was, if I could manage to keep the stepmonster from taking the 'Vette away from me.

Tony raised his eyes to look into mine. "You're impossible to say 'no' to. I just can't help but think I'll end up in jail or worse by dating you."

I shook my head. "I haven't been in jail yet. Well, unless you count the odd hour here or there before the stepmonster came to bail me out. That's one good thing about coming from a family with money. My mom's lawyer is one scary bastard. Judges usually let me off with a slap on the wrist just to get him out of their courtroom."

Tony laughed and raised his head off my shoulder. "You're impossible. I never know if you're telling a tall tale or the truth. And the scary thing is, I think it's the truth. I should run away from you, but all I want to do is make love to you."

I leaned back, running a hand over the bed. "We seem to be in the perfect place for lovemaking."

"Do you have any condoms on you? I didn't bring any."

I didn't, and I didn't feel like running down to my room. The mood would be shattered. "There's lots of things we can do with mouth and hand that don't require a condom." I pulled him back, so that we were both lying on the bed, our legs dangling off the edge. "Would you like a demonstration?"

"Yes, please," he replied with a laugh. He leaned in to kiss me but stopped abruptly. "Did you hear that?"

"Hear what?"

"I thought I heard something moving."

"Bedsprings squeaking, I think."

"Seemed to be coming from the corner. Like, right under the bed."

"Perhaps Winston Manor has mice." I leaned my face in until our noses were touching. "Let's forget mice and fiancées and everything else for right now. Right now is just for the two of us. No intruders need apply."

We kissed and groped and moaned a bit. Before long our pants were undone and we were stroking each other, and the kisses were getting more and more intense. We released the grip on our respective cocks long enough for Tony to shift himself around so that he was lying on the bed properly. Idiot that I am, I wanted to show off my athleticism, so I placed one hand on the bed and vaulted myself onto it, pretty much landing right on top of him. It would have been impressive if the bed had been stronger. The damn thing broke as my weight landed, one of the legs at the bottom snapping, making the whole thing slope. Worse, it made a tremendous crash.

"Oops," I said.

Tony laughed. "It's never dull with you." He kissed me and held me tight.

The kiss was interrupted by voices on the stairs. It seemed the breaking of the bed had been heard, and people were coming to investigate. I heard one voice in particular saying, "The sound came from up here, I tell you." It was my stepmonster.

"Shit!" I cursed under my breath. The voice was close, and I knew Tony and I wouldn't have time to pull up our pants and do up the belts and not look like we had been engaged in hanky panky before the door opened to reveal all. "Quick! Under the bed!"

We both rolled off the mattress and onto the floor. I heard the click of the doorknob just as we were sliding ourselves backward and under the bed. I was on the broken end, and I pushed up with my shoulders, holding the bed up enough so that the broken leg wouldn't be noticed. It wasn't comfortable, but it was necessary.

I could see legs entering. "The light's on. Someone's been in here," my stepmonster said.

"Doesn't seem to be anyone here now," replied another set of legs. The voice belonged to Mark Winston.

"Not a ghost, at any case. Look over there. Wine bottle and glasses."

I couldn't see him doing it, but I could sense movement from Tony, who was slowly moving, pulling up his pants. It seemed a good idea, but I couldn't manage to do the same with my shoulders holding up the bed. I was pretty much stuck in the all-fours position. I held my breath. It seemed inevitable that at any moment Dollings would look under the bed and see our lovely faces.

"That bang came from in here, I swear it." Dollings was pacing around. I could imagine his nostrils quivering as he tried to pick up a scent like a bloodhound. "I can't see anything amiss, though."

"Might have been the house settling," suggested Winston.

"That loud crash?"

"It's a big house."

"That was no house settling. It sounded like someone taking a sledgehammer to some furniture."

There was some movement around my legs. I frowned and turned my head, as much as I could it with it being jammed up against the bedsprings, to glare at Tony. Much as I liked him, I didn't think we were in the right time or place to play footsie. I was surprised to note that he seemed not to be moving at all. He had yanked his pants up but hadn't dared to fasten his belt, rightly thinking the sound would be heard by Dollings and Winston. I could make out Tony's huddled shape, and he had pulled himself into almost a fetal position. His hands were around his knees, which meant that his feet were fairly distant from mine. What was fiddling around with my pant leg, then?

Whatever it was worked its way into my pants and proceeded to slowly crawl up my leg. I felt the little legs and realized I'd located Ernie's tarantula.

Chapter Fifteen

A FACT about tarantulas: while their bite is venomous, it won't kill anything larger than itself, generally speaking. It's a bit like a bee sting. Unpleasant, but bearable. They're also, like any arachnid, terribly easy to kill, owing to the squash factor. Some of them, little Jeffrey included, can move quite quickly. Jeffrey had crawled up my calf with amazing speed. However, once he got to my knee he stopped, undoubtedly puzzled by the fact that his route had been blocked by scrunched up denim and knee. Unless he wanted to really work at it and shift around some of the material, he'd gone as far as he could.

Knowing that the bite of a tarantula isn't deadly doesn't help one when one of the little beggars has crawled up your pants leg. Any creature shuffling around the leg hairs is bound to make you feel like jumping up and doing a dance until the bastard drops out, the other option being to smack it with your hand, getting arachnid innards all over your leg. I couldn't jump up without alerting the stepmonster of my presence, and I didn't want to squish Jeffrey because he was a pet, even if it was to an unpleasant brute like Ernie. So I bit my lip.

"Did you hear that?" Dollings asked.

Winston said that he heard nothing.

"Sounded like something making a high-pitched gasp."

Okay, so I made a little sound before I bit my lip. Tarantulas strolling up your leg will do that to a guy. But I objected to the "high-pitched" bit. It was a manly intake of breath, if anything.

Dollings had stopped his pacing a mere foot away from my nose. And of course he then did what I prayed he wouldn't. He sat on the bed.

The sudden weight over my head and shoulders, added to the distress felt by Jeffrey, proved too much for the Weasley muscles. I sank, and naturally the bed sank as well. Dollings let out a small cry—definitely high-pitched and unmanly—as the bed tilted.

"What the blazes?" he shouted.

The commotion had one good benefit. Jeffrey, thinking there was too much noise around and realizing he wasn't going to gain farther access up my leg, decided to do an about-face and scurry back down my leg.

Tony grabbed my hand and leaned into me, quickly whispering, "Stay here." And before I could protest, he scooted out from under the bed.

His sudden appearance made Dollings stand up in surprise, thankfully saving my head and right shoulder from further squashing. I watched as Tony rose to his feet and dusted off the knees of his pants. After that, it was like watching a play with really, really bad seats. All I could see were three sets of legs.

"What were you doing under the bed?" Winston demanded.

Dollings, not wanting to let someone else get all the yelling in, piped up as well. "Just what is going on around here?"

There was an uncomfortable pause as Tony tried to think of an explanation. He stammered a bit.

"Well?" Dollings asked.

Jeffrey, wanting to get a better look, I suppose, had crawled up and was near my face. I gave the hairy spider a little push, causing him to scuttle out into view. Thankfully Tony spotted the little guy. "I was looking for Ernie's spider."

"Why in tarnation would Ernie's spider be up here?"

"I don't know. Perhaps you should ask him. He's right by your leg."

The stepmonster yelped and danced quickly away from Jeffrey. The spider flexed a leg or two, probably stretching after the confined space inside my pant leg, but otherwise showed no offense at Dollings's rude behavior. I imagine Jeffrey also rolled all eight eyes in exasperation, wondering how humans could be so jumpy.

"I saw him coming in under the door," Tony said, warming to his story. "I was meeting a friend up here and we were going to watch the sun set and drink some wine, and there was Jeffrey, darting under the door. I got in and searched for him. Unfortunately I broke the leg off the bed when I was trying to get at him. I had crawled under the bed to retrieve him when you came in."

"Why didn't you let us know you were here?" Winston asked.

The question would have stumped me, but Tony was a fast thinker. "I nearly had Jeffrey and didn't want to startle him. Once I realized he'd crawl out on his own when he got bored with being under the bed, I slid back out."

Tony was good. He spoke with authority, making his lie believable. I believed him, and I knew he was making the whole thing up. It certainly convinced Winston and Dollings.

"Yes, well, we heard a crash coming from in here," Winston said, his tone now congenial instead of accusatory. "I thought that maybe burglars had gotten in and were lying in wait until the household had gone to bed before making off with my Zopfi."

"And the silver," Dollings added.

"No burglars," Tony said. "Just spider hunters."

"How are we going to get that… thing back downstairs?" Dollings asked. "I'm certainly not picking up the vile thing."

"Don't look at me." Winston's tone was sour. "I don't want to touch it."

"The tarantula probably feels the same way," Tony said. His legs moved around the room, and I could hear him rummaging around for something. "This should do. We can keep him in this jar long enough to get him back to his owner."

Tony crouched down to scoop the spider into the jar he'd found, managing to flash me a wink before getting back to his feet.

"Who was it," Winston wondered, "that you were meeting up here?"

"Sorry?"

"You said that you were meeting a friend up here to watch the sunset."

"Oh. Weasel. Patrick Weasley."

I heard Dollings grunt. "That explains the wine. My stepson drinks like a fish."

"Let's get this… thing… back to Ernie," suggested Winston, "before it gets out of that jar."

"I say we should crush it and just let him believe it couldn't be found," the stepmonster said. "A spider is hardly a good pet for a child to have."

Gee, stepdad. Whatever happened to "all creatures great and small"? I was glad he'd moved away from the bed because I had the sudden urge to bite his ankles.

The three pair of legs walked away, and I heard the door to the nursery open and close. I stayed, unmoving, until I could no longer hear their footsteps retreating down the stairs before sliding out from under the bed. I dusted myself off and then strode over to the door.

The knob refused to turn. Whoever had gone out last had locked the door behind them.

I rattled the knob, which was foolish because I knew the door was indeed locked. People do that, though, hoping the door will go, "Hey! I was just kidding. I'm not really locked. Come on out!" This door remained silent and locked. I examined the door. It was old but solid. The lock worked by a key, and an examination of the mechanism showed me the key was still in the lock.

What idiot locks the door of a nursery that isn't even used anymore? Obviously it had been either Dollings or Winston. I preferred to believe it was Dollings, just because I already didn't like him.

Luckily, I was a mystery reader, and I knew what to do. You slide a sheet of paper under the door and then, using a hat pin, push the key out of the lock. The key falls onto the paper and you pull the paper back and—voila!—you have the key. I didn't have a hat pin, but I was sure I could find something suitable.

I searched the room and found an old newspaper (very old, the headline informed me that Reagan had been elected to his second term) and a thickish bit of wire I figured would be stiff enough to shove the key out of the lock.

Step one: easy. The newspaper went right under the door. Step two: also easy. The wire worked like a charm and I heard the key fall right onto the paper. Step three is where it all fell apart. Apparently in all those old mysteries, there's room enough beneath the door for a key to slide through. This door was designed to allow newspapers to slide easily from one side to the other, but not keys. So while I was still locked in the room, I could read all about Reagan's defeat of Walter Mondale.

I sat on the floor for a while, glaring at the door. The door glared back.

Surely Tony would return and let me out, I thought. As the minutes ticked away, though, I began to think something or someone was preventing him from doing so.

Luckily, there was still the bottle of wine.

TONY and I had been more interested in each other than the wine, so we had barely had a sip or two before abandoning it. I finished what was in his glass first, then polished off mine. Then I forgot the glasses and drank directly from the bottle.

Halfway through the bottle, I had a really stupid idea.

Three quarters of the way through the bottle, the idea didn't seem so stupid any longer and I got up to check out the window. The windows in the tower opened sideways, like little doors. I tried mine. It opened easily. The sun had given it up for the day and the moon was a no-show, so it was pretty hard to make out details. There was no ledge, that much I could see. I looked up. A monkey might be able to climb out of the window and make it to the roof, and Spider-Man would have laughed at my dilemma, but I was neither a monkey nor had I been bitten by a radioactive spider. I looked sideways. Curved walls both ways, with no footholds or handholds visible. There was a drainpipe coming down from the roof, but it was out of reach. I looked down. If I lowered myself, I might be able to reach the next floor down—if I was eight feet tall.

I wasn't drunk enough, so I went back and finished the bottle of wine. That done, I went back to the window. There was a cool breeze and one of those misty sort of rains going on, and I didn't have a jacket, so whatever I decided to do, I'd want to do it quickly. Clinging to the side of a house isn't fun, but it's less fun if you're cold.

I got up on the windowsill and peered down into the gloom. There was a patio below me. Cement. Not good. "Don't fall, Weasel old son," I told myself. Next to the patio was the Winston swimming pool, but if I fell from where I was, I'd splat several yards away from the water. Awkwardly I turned around on the sill and perched on my knees. I took a deep breath and then started to lower myself out of the window.

I think I was assuming there would be some foothold I would find that I hadn't seen. There wasn't. My feet dangled down to the window below, but there was nowhere for them to get a grip. Anyone looking out that window would just see my size 12 Nikes hanging there.

Realizing I had done something incredibly stupid, for which I blamed the wine (it was Australian), I tried to pull myself back up, only to find I couldn't. Panic set in. I knew my fingers wouldn't be able to hold me there for too long a time. "Um," I said, "help!"

My feet tapped against the window below me. Luckily, someone heard the tapping, and in a moment, I heard someone undo the latch, swing the window open, and say, "What the hell?"

It was Caps. "Hey, buddy," I said, trying to sound nonchalant, "I could use a hand here."

"What the hell are you doing?" he demanded.

"Well, I'm pretty certain I'm drunk and about to fall to my certain doom unless you help me out!"

My fingers were getting numb. I looked down to see his puzzled face looking up at me. "You're going to hurt yourself doing things like this! Why don't you scramble up and get in the way you went out?"

"The thought had occurred to me, but I'm dangling by my fingertips. Not enough purchase for hauling purposes. In fact, if you don't grab hold of my feet very quickly, I may do a Humpty Dumpty!"

Caps got up onto the sill of his window and reached up to catch my feet. "Now what?" he asked.

"Hold them tight, you ass!"

"No need to yell, you know!" he protested.

I gazed down at the patio. "I'm pretty sure there is!"

"I hate to say this, Weasel," he said, "but if you let go, we're both probably going to fall. Can you lower yourself any further?"

"Nope. Any suggestions?"

"Can you get over to that drainpipe?"

It was out of reach, but with Caps holding on to my feet, all I had to do was swing sideways and I'd be able to grasp it. "I think I can."

Caps, crouched on his sill, pushed himself up as much as he could. "Are you sure you can do this?"

"Yes, although that could be the Pinot Grigio talking."

Tightening his grip on my ankles, Caps said, through clenched teeth, "Okay, anytime you're ready."

As my fingers were about to give out, I was ready. I let go, pushing myself off to the side. I screamed. Caps screamed. My arms reached out. My eyes were closed because I felt certain I was going to fall to my death. I knew where, in a general way, the drainpipe was, so I grabbed. I was surprised when my hands grasped metal. Shocked, I opened my eyes, thinking it was some passing bit of metal I was feeling and not the spout and that in seconds I would be splatting against the pavement. No, it really was the drainpipe. I held onto that sucker for dear life.

Drunk but alive and not splatted, I was feeling pretty good. Caps was still yelling, and I noticed I had something heavy hanging from me.

Caps hadn't released me. He had come with me, falling out of the window, and was now clinging to my ankles.

"You were supposed to let go, you ass!" I yelled.

"I lost my balance! It was that or fall!"

My hands were grasping the pipe just above where a bracket was bolted into the masonry. The combined weight of both me and Caps wasn't doing the drainpipe any good. It had obviously been there for ages, and the bolts were shaking a little, the grout around them crumbling. "Um, Caps," I said.

"Yes?"

"We may be doing a little falling anyway."

"What do you—"

The rest of Caps's sentence was a scream as the drainpipe broke off from the gutter surrounding the roof and we fell away from the wall. "This is going to hurt!" I cried out. I was just glad I was drunk. Being drunk takes the edge off dying.

Imagine my surprise when we hit water.

Chapter Sixteen

WE WERE in Caps's room, drying ourselves with towels and finding clothes that weren't soaked. Since they were Caps's clothes, he didn't have any trouble, but I'm a bit taller than he is, and the only jeans he had for me made me look like Huck Finn.

"Don't you have anything longer?" I asked.

"This isn't Macy's. There's still the Gray Lady getup in the bathroom. You could always wear that."

I sighed. "This will do. How about socks?"

While he rummaged in his drawer for socks, I sat on his bed and contemplated several things, the main one being whether I was going to throw up. If you've ever swung off a broken drainpipe with your belly full of wine and fallen into the deep end of a pool, you'll be familiar with the feeling. On the one hand, I wanted to sit and marvel over how we had swung somewhat to the side, therefore not hitting hard pavement, but on the other hand, my body wanted to upchuck. The body won. I quickly rose from the bed and darted for the bathroom, poising my head over the toilet just in time.

"Are you getting sick in there?" Caps asked.

I couldn't answer with anything other than a noisy heave.

"You'd better not get any of your sick on my jeans. They're fairly new."

His jeans weren't high on my list of things to worry about, although how he thought my sick was going to fly out of the toilet and despoil his jeans was beyond me. After what seemed to be about a year and a half but was probably only a minute or so, I rose. I washed my face in the sink and padded back to sit on the bed.

"I'll need a T-shirt, too." My voice was thick, but I was feeling slightly better. I just wished the mariachi band in my head would tone it down a little. I shook my head and immediately regretted it. I pressed my fingers against my temples to keep my brain from bursting out of my skull. "I can't believe no one heard us. We must have made a hell of a splash."

"Big house. Most everyone was on the other side playing cards."

"What time is it?"

"Just about one thirty."

"Late enough," I said, rising. "Let's check and see if everyone has gone to bed, and get this thing over with."

"First we've got to fix that pipe."

I gaped at him. "Whatever for? It obviously didn't want to be clinging to the wall any longer. I say leave it be."

"I don't want my uncle to see it all bent like it is. We at least need to get it back up against the wall so it isn't stretched out across the patio."

So out we went. The rain had increased, and the wind had whipped up considerably. Off in the distance, we could hear the rumble of storm clouds. Not wanting to get soaked again, we worked quickly. I can't say we did a good job, but we did get the pipe back up so that it was somewhat close to the wall. It still wasn't connected to the gutter, nor was it bracketed to the wall, but it would have to do until Caps could call some repairmen to mend or replace it.

We stood looking up at our handiwork.

"It's not exactly right," I said honestly.

"No," he agreed. "It's closer to the nursery window than it was."

"And it's not against the wall. The house looks like it's got a hangnail."

Caps hugged himself as the wind howled around us. "It'll do for now. Let's get inside and get that will swapped. Still have it with you?"

"Stuck it in the back pocket."

"Then let's get this over with."

We returned inside and went up to the second floor to see if anyone seemed to be up and about. Everything seemed quiet. Moving as silently as we could, Caps went down one end of the hall and I went down the other, listening at doors to hear if anyone was stirring. Nothing. We met back near the center, and I whispered, "Seems good."

"I guess the badminton wore them out," Caps agreed.

"We'll check downstairs just to make sure, and then you watch the library door and I'll swap the wills. Be done in three minutes."

I spoke too soon. As we crept toward the west staircase, we heard footsteps coming up. Guiltily, Caps and I froze, me with one foot poised over the top step. I breathed a sigh of relief when Tony came around the corner onto the landing. He smiled when he saw me.

"I was just coming to see if you were still up," he said.

Caps and I both shushed him as we trod down the steps to meet him on the landing. "We don't want to disturb anyone," I told him. "Is anyone downstairs that you saw?"

Tony shook his head. "I think everyone's asleep. Exciting crowd. I think the badminton wore them out."

Caps nodded. "That's what I said." He frowned as I kissed Tony's pretty face. "Um, isn't this the guy my uncle hired to serve meals?"

I smiled and grabbed Tony's hand. "Yeah, this is Tony. Tony, this is my friend, Caps. Tony and I like each other, Caps."

"I kind of gathered that."

The three of us went down the rest of the stairs while Tony— still a little too loudly for my liking—asked, "Where have you been? I've been looking all over for you ever since I finally got away from your stepfather and that beastly spider."

"I was locked in the nursery for ages," I said.

Having reached the bottom of the stairs, Tony turned to me and gave me a sorrowful look. "I knew something was wrong. Mr. Winston must have locked it on his way out. I was deputized to return the spider to the kid, and it took me forever to get away. The little brat was so thankful that his pet had been returned, and he told me everything I never wanted to know about tarantulas. Once I got away, I went up to your room. When you weren't there, I looked around, finally going back to the nursery. You weren't there."

"No, by then I'd drunk the whole bottle of wine and had climbed out the window."

"You could have hurt yourself!"

"He could have hurt me!" Caps said. I shushed him. Really, these guys had no clue as to how to conduct a stealth operation. True, Tony didn't *know* he was involved in a stealth operation, but you'd think with all the shushing, people would get a clue.

"I'll tell you all about it later," I told Tony, "but for now, I wonder if you'd do a favor for me? Would you stand up on the landing and watch for anyone coming downstairs? If you see anyone, signal to Caps. He'll be keeping watch at the door to the library."

Tony shrugged. "Sure. What for?"

I brandished the envelope containing the will. "I'm just going to swap this old will and put it in the safe in place of the new will."

"Um... that sounds really, really illegal."

"Probably is. That's why we'd like you to keep an eye on the stairs."

"But this isn't the only staircase! What if someone comes down from the east end of the house, or by the back stairs?"

"They're further away from the library and Caps will see them in plenty of time. This staircase is close to the library, and having you give us an early warning will be helpful. I'll explain everything later."

Tony blinked and then shook his head. "I knew you were going to land me in jail. I just didn't think it would be this soon."

I gave him a playful smack on the arm. "There's a good chap. Really, this will just take a minute. With everyone asleep, what can possibly go wrong?"

Caps groaned. "I wish you hadn't said that."

With Tony keeping watch on the stairs, Caps and I made for the library. We opted for not turning on the lights, but I did switch on the little flashlight I'd brought with me. The storm outside had finally hit, and every now and then the room was lit by a brilliant flash of lightning. Rain was pelting against the French windows.

"Whistle if you see anyone," I told Caps.

He nodded.

I walked over to the portrait of Charlotte Winston and swung it aside. Holding the flashlight in my left hand, I made quick work of the locking mechanism. Hitting the last number, I reached for the handle but stopped before opening the safe door. I looked behind me. I could have sworn I'd heard a sound that hadn't been thunder or Caps's labored breathing. I looked over to the door. Caps had heard it too. I could see his dark form, pointing to a chair in the corner.

Shining my flashlight in that direction, I could see a huddled form attempting, badly, to conceal himself behind the chair. The trouble was it wasn't a particularly large chair and it was a large form, so whole blobs of the form stuck out. I trained the beam onto the form's face to reveal our interloper. It was Tyler Kendrick, who rose with a sheepish smile.

"Hi, guys," he said lamely.

"What," I asked, "are you doing hiding behind a chair in the dark?"

"What are you doing going through the library with flashlights?" he asked in return.

"We asked first," Caps said.

I had an answer, though. "We were ghost hunting."

"So was I," Kendrick said unconvincingly.

I played the flashlight beam over him. "Why do you have that envelope in your hand?"

He held up the item in question. It was a thick envelope and looked a hell of a lot like the one currently residing in my back pocket. "This?" he said, trying to look dismissive. "This is nothing."

I took a few steps toward him. "It has writing on it. Last will and testament."

"Does it?" He looked at the envelope. "I just found this lying on the floor."

I fixed an arched eyebrow in his direction. Realizing we were in the dark and he had a flashlight in his eyes, making me just a marvelous dark shape in his path and my facial expressions lost on him, I held out my hand. "Let me see that."

Kendrick seemed to deflate like a balloon at a kid's party. "Look, I'll level with you. I came down here to switch this will with the one in the safe."

"Say what?" Caps asked.

Sighing heavily, Kendrick went around and sank into the chair he'd been crouching behind. Putting his face in his hands, he said, "Look, I know I've never been the best of friends to either of you guys—"

"You used to give me swirlies in high school," I reminded him.

Kendrick ignored this reminder of our past. "Truth is, I'm glad you caught me. I've been torn with guilt ever since I came up with this stupid scheme. You see, I planned to switch this will with her new one in the safe. Can I confide in you, Weasel? And you, Caps?"

I thought using our nicknames was a cheap ploy, smacking too much of "hey, we're all just really good friends, aren't we, fellas?" Ordinarily I would have uttered a hollow laugh and told him to stick a sock in it, but I wanted to hear his tale. I switched off the flashlight just as a flash of lightning lit the room momentarily. It seemed to me that I saw a tear making its way down Kendrick's cheek, but I could have been mistaken. "Go on," I said.

"Um, do we have to sit here in the dark?" Kendrick asked. "With all those noises outside, and the thunder and lightning and stuff, it's a bit eerie. And do you think I could have a drink?"

I nodded to Caps and he must have at least been able to make out the movement of my head because seconds later the lights came on. There was a brandy decanter on the sideboard, and I went over and found there was a little bit left, so I poured Kendrick a snifter. He swallowed it in one go and visibly shuddered before composing himself.

"That hits the spot," he said with a weak laugh.

"The will," I said, reminding him this wasn't a social gathering.

Kendrick continued reluctantly. "In the last few months of her life, Mrs. Winston and I became pretty good friends—"

"You had an affair with a cougar," I said, cutting to the chase.

Nodding, Kendrick held out the brandy snifter, probably thinking I'd give him more. There wasn't any, so I just took the glass from him and set it aside. "I knew she liked me. You can tell. The way she watched me when I mowed the lawns, that sort of thing. She'd call me into the house a lot, offering me something to drink." He gazed at his empty glass I'd set on the coffee table as if it might magically refill. "She'd get me some lemonade or something and made sure she brushed up against me a lot."

I winced, hoping he wasn't going to go into too much detail. I really didn't want to hear about Kendrick and Charlotte Winston bumping uglies.

"She made her intentions obvious. Finally, one day when Mr. Winston was away, she asked me to go up to her room with her."

I think I heard Caps make a gagging sound.

"I was reluctant," Kendrick said, either not hearing or ignoring the sound, "but she was pretty persistent. Then she said that if I became her lover, she'd be sure to mention me in her will. If I was really good to her, she said she would even go as far as to leave me a million dollars."

"Wow," I said. "Didn't she know she could have had a really good-looking hooker for much, much less?"

"She wanted someone close by and someone she could have often."

"Again. Hooker. Much, much less. Just saying."

Kendrick didn't argue the point. "Anyway, I became her lover. And true to her word, she said she had a new will made out. And then one day she found my cell phone lying around, and she checked my text messages. Seeing a lot of flirting with some girls I was seeing at the time, she got mad. She didn't talk to me for days, and then she called me into the library. She told me she'd had a new will made out and gave me the old one, the one giving me a million dollars, to destroy. She laughed as she handed it to me."

"This sounds oddly familiar," Caps said. I hushed him.

Kendrick went on. "I don't know why I kept this will. I certainly didn't have any idea at the time that I'd try to swap wills, but I held onto it. Then she died, and the idea came to me. I mean, I deserve something for—"

I waved my hands, not wanting to hear anything more. "And you never opened the envelope?"

He shook his head. "It'd be a bunch of legal stuff I wouldn't understand. Why open it?"

I held out my hand, and he passed over the envelope. He squeaked a protest as I slit it open. Inside there were several sheets of thick paper. At first I thought they were all blank, but the last page had writing on it. A lavender ink had been used, and the handwriting was scrawled and difficult to make out. I read the missive to myself first. As a writer, Charlotte Winston was no Danielle Steele. She wasn't even a Dan Brown, and if Dan Brown were off his rocker enough to have an affair with Tyler Kendrick, he couldn't even lower himself to C. Winston level. The handwriting could have been that of a child, especially if said child were writing with her feet. There were lots of cross-outs and blurred letters, so it was hard going.

By the time I'd gotten to the end, Caps couldn't stand the suspense. "What does it say?"

I read it aloud.

Dear Kendrick: I have no idea if you'll ever read this. Certainly if you do as you were instructed, you won't read it and will have destroyed it, but it's been my experience that you often do not do what you're told to do. You really are a stupid, stupid man. There never was a will leaving you a million dollars. If you truly believed that I'd do anything that ridiculous, you're far more delusional than I thought you were. My copy of my real will is where it has always been, in the safe behind my portrait. I'm wondering how long it will be before you break down in tears and come to me, begging me for forgiveness. Perhaps you won't. Perhaps you really will destroy this. Or maybe you'll…something illegible… and open the envelope to read this, just to see what could have been yours. It will be fun watching you squirm. I may be an ill woman and I may not get the enjoyment out of life that I once… I'm assuming the word is got, but it looks more like goat… but giving you this envelope will give me hours of pleasure. How long will it be before you crumble? My guess is within a few days, but you might surprise me. You've certainly surprised me in bed. I thought you would have been better.

It was signed simply Char.

There was an uncomfortable silence after I'd finished reading, finally broken by Kendrick.

"I never was going to get a million dollars?"

He sounded like a kid who had just found out Santa wasn't real. No one answered him. I dropped Kendrick's "will" onto the table next to his glass and reached into my back pocket for the will Winston had given me, a sinking feeling in my heart. Slowly I opened this envelope. Again, I found several blank pages and one handwritten one. I read it aloud.

Mark: You always were a very foolish man. Did you really think that I would bequeath our gardener a large sum of money? I know you and I have always had our differences and don't really get along, but please! How stupid do you think I am? I may not have loved you, but I love this house and

you need the money to keep it up after I'm gone,
since you seem to have squandered the money left
you by your family. I'm amusing myself
wondering how long before you open this or try
something silly, like swapping this envelope with
the real will in the safe. That would be hilarious! I
may not like you, Mark dear, but you do amuse me.
And giving you this fake document will provide
me with days of amusement, watching you squirm.

Again, it was signed Char.

This time the uncomfortable silence was broken by Caps, who muttered, "Well, that's a piss down the leg!"

"The woman really liked the word 'squirm'. Not only did she use it in both letters, but she wrote the word all over the back of this one, with lots of exclamation points," I said.

Tony came in, looking puzzled. "I wondered what was taking so long. You said you'd be—"

I let the papers slip from my lifeless fingers. "Oh, we've just been in here, being made fun of by a dead woman. Charlotte Winston's having a good laugh from beyond the grave, watching us run around like idiots."

"I don't understand."

"Tell you later. Suffice to say, the need for you keep watch on the stairs is now kaput. On the plus side, though, you and I can go upstairs, and you can make me forget Charlotte Winston and her spurious wills ever existed."

Kendrick, who had been sitting in a stunned stupor, raised his head to look at me. "Wait. Were you trying to swap wills, too?"

"It had seemed like a good idea."

"So that was you rattling the French windows outside earlier? Why didn't you just come in from the hall?"

"You mentioned noises outside earlier. Must just have been the storm. We arrived just moments before finding you skulking behind the chair."

Kendrick frowned. "No, I heard someone scuffling outside, I'm sure of it. It even seemed like I heard whispering, but it was hard to hear over the rain. Then someone rattled the doorknobs on the French windows. That's when I ducked behind the chair. I thought someone was coming in and I'd be caught."

"I thought you hid when we came in."

"No, you came in shortly after the rattling."

I shrugged. "Well, if it wasn't the wind or rain, it must have been one of the ghosts of Winston Manor. No one else would be out on a night like this."

Caps wasn't worried about rattling doors or much of anything. He stood near the door, shaking his head sadly. "In the past two days, I've fallen down the stairs, I've been dunked into cold water twice, and I've dangled off the side of the house, but this—*this*—sucks!" He let out a growl and moved past Tony to exit the room. "I'm going to bed. Maybe when I wake up, I'll find this has all been a bad dream."

He was only out of sight for a second or so before we heard a thumping sound, and then Caps fell back into our view, hitting the carpeted floor like a rag doll. "Caps?" I said. I started toward the door but stopped as two men entered. One of them held a blackjack, which must have been what caused Caps to collapse. The other held a gun. Both of them wore ski masks, so I couldn't really see their faces, but I had the impression they weren't happy fellows. The one with the gun pointed it straight at Tony, who immediately backed up and put his hands in the air.

"No one move," the one with the gun growled. "And no one make a sound."

Chapter Seventeen

NO ONE moved. I'm not sure this was entirely because of the threat. On my own part, I remained still because I was sure it was a joke and the two goons in the doorway were at any moment going to pull off their ski masks to show us that it was Papa Dollings and Mark Winston. The stepmonster, I knew from past experience, was only free from the nuthouse by loopholes in its criteria, and the Winston family obviously had a streak of insanity. Look at poor old Charlotte, whose idea of a good time was fucking Kendrick and passing around fake wills.

So we stood in tableau for what seemed hours, although I'm sure it wasn't. When the thugs didn't doff their caps with a hearty, "Surprise! It was us all along!", it finally sank in that these two guys might be actual burglars. Realizing the gun fixed on Tony's chest might not be of the water-squirting variety, I took an involuntarily step toward him. The protective instinct in me, I suppose. I didn't get far before the guy turned and pointed his gun at me. "I said nobody move!"

I stopped. Kendrick seemed to have only just registered that two more had joined the party. He blinked. "What's going on here?"

"Shut up," the one with the blackjack barked. I think he was trying to be intimidating, but he sounded a lot like Curly from the

Three Stooges, and even with him armed with a blackjack, it's hard to be scared of Curly from the Three Stooges. He must have realized this, because he pocketed the blackjack and pulled out a gun of his own. He trained his between Kendrick and Tony. His eyes were the only facial feature we could see, and he darted his little piggy eyes over at his companion. "What are all these people doing here? I thought you said everyone would be asleep."

"I guess our info was incorrect," the other said. "I thought there would only be a few people living here and that all we'd have to do was break in and get the picture." He jabbed his gun in the air. "Come on, you. Put 'em up."

I raised my hands, as did Kendrick. I'd always wondered if crooks really said "Put 'em up" like they did in the movies. Now I knew. Go figure.

I thought Kendrick, being a cop, might show a little backbone and throw a Chuck Norris-style quip to the gun-toting duo. You know the sort of thing. "You guys should have brought bigger guns" or "You call those guns? *These* are guns." And then his biceps would burst out of his shirt like the Incredible Hulk, and he'd go all kung fu on their asses. Instead he seemed to try to sink into his seat cushion in an attempt to make his big body invisible.

Tony showed bravery by asking, "What do you want?" His voice shook only slightly.

"We're here to get the picture," the one who sounded like Curly replied. He pronounced it "pitcher."

"The Zopfi," the other added.

"You're saying it wrong," I said. "It rhymes with softy. The soft I at the end." I lowered my hands slightly.

It occurred to me that these were not expert burglars. If it had been them Kendrick had heard outside earlier, and I could hardly believe that more thieves were out on such a stormy night, they had totally failed to gain access through the French windows, which couldn't have had very difficult locks on them. After their epic fail with the French windows, they had apparently searched elsewhere for easier access, such as an unlocked window. Real burglars would 1: know how to jimmy a lock, 2: have realized that, with all the cars parked around the garage, the house was full and that bumping into the odd person or two might occur, and 3: know how to pronounce the artist of the painting they were there to steal.

I don't claim to be psychic, but even without seeing the faces, I suddenly knew the identity of our thieves. We were being held at gunpoint by the Smothers brothers. The shapes of their bodies were right, and besides, I recalled the jacket Curly was wearing was identical to the one Brandon Smothers—I hadn't known which brother was which until Mark told me—had worn when I first met them.

Know thy enemy, someone famous had once said. I think it was Richard Nixon, but I could be mistaken about that. Regardless, I now knew my enemy and I knew they were idiots. True, they were idiots with guns, but somehow they were less frightening now.

"I don't care if it's a fucking Picasso, we're here to steal it!" the one I now knew to be Howard said.

I lowered my hands the rest of the way. "Steal away," I said nonchalantly.

Both of them stared at me. "Huh?" Brandon asked.

"Steal it. Take it away. Remove it from the premises. Be my guest." I went for a relaxed pose. If I were a smoker, I'd have lit up a cigarette. It would have been a cool movie moment. Very David Niven.

Howard squinted his eyes. "What gives?"

I shrugged. "Nothing. You've got guns. We can't stop you. The painting is right there on the wall. It's the landscape, not the portrait. The signature in the bottom right corner reads 'A. Zopfi.' I think his first name was Anthony, but it may have been Andrew or even Ambrose. Art was never my field of expertise, although even I...."

Drawing on my acting skills—did I mention that I'd played Jumbo the Elephant in the third grade class play?—I suddenly stopped and looked guilty, like I'd begun to say something I shouldn't have said.

Brandon pointed at the picture above the mantelpiece. "This picture? This the one?" Burglar tip number 4: don't point with your gun. Use your free hand. Gun should stay pointed at your victims.

"Wait a minute," his brother said. His gun stayed fixed, the muzzle right in line with my heart. He'd obviously gone over the list of burglar tips before setting off on their caper. "Is there something wrong with that picture?"

"Oh, no," I said, making sure it came out a little quickly. "Perfectly fine. Nothing wrong with it at all."

Howard strode toward me, the gun now aimed at my head. I have to admit, the barrel looked really, really large, and I could only imagine the size of the bullet that would come out if he pulled the trigger. "Come on, you," he snarled. "Give. What's wrong with that picture?"

I hung my head in defeat. "If you must know, we just learned that it's a fake. Mr. Winston invited an art expert here for the weekend. He's upstairs right now, sleeping the sleep of the just, and he told us that the Zopfi is a fake."

"What do you mean, a fake?" Brandon squeaked.

"I mean it was painted by A. Ziglar, A. Zimmerman, A. Ziggy, or anyone but A. Zopfi. It's a really pretty picture, but not," I said, shaking my head sadly, "worth the canvas it's painted on. Mind you, it's a good forgery. Mark Winston's pretty knowledgeable about such things, and it fooled him."

Howard, frowning but keeping his gun pointed generally in my direction, moved closer to the painting. "This one? It's a fake?"

"None faker."

"It's called *Man With Gazelle,* and it's supposed to be by this Zopfi guy?" He got the pronunciation right.

"That's the one. Look closely. The artist, whoever he was, messed up on the gazelle. Looks more like a weird dog."

"Keep 'em covered," he told his brother. I thought for a second he was even going to call his partner "Brandon," giving away the whole game. Brandon stood, pointing his gun from me to Kendrick to Tony and then back to me while Howard got up close to the picture. He nearly put his nose to the canvas. "Yeah," he said, "I see what you mean. He did mess up the gazelle."

As unprofessional as these two goons were, I couldn't get them to lower their guard enough for me to make a move. I'm quick, but I'm not that quick. Maybe, just maybe, if I could convince them there was no valuable painting to steal, they would just leave.

"So what do we do?" Brandon asked.

"We steal everything we can find. Dad—I mean, our boss—won't like it, but there's no sense in stealing this picture if it's no good. Got the cords? We'll need to gag and tie these idiots up."

Damn. I needed to either get the Smothers brothers to make a mistake, which I was sure they'd do if given enough time, or get them somewhere where I could lock them in. Somewhere like…

The nursery room in the tower. The key should still be in the lock. If I could convince them there was something worth stealing up there, I could lead them up there and lock them in.

Brandon had several lengths of cord stuffed away in an inside pocket of his jacket. He pulled them out and dropped them onto the floor and then strode over to Tony and grabbed him roughly by the elbow, using enough force to make Tony yelp out a protest.

"Don't worry, Tony," I said quickly, "they won't find the…." I shut my mouth tightly as if I'd said too much again.

"Won't find what?" Howard again pointed his gun at my skull. "What are you afraid we'll find?"

I slumped my shoulders in defeat. "Mark Winston just acquired a valuable Ernie Boone painting. He had the art expert examine it as well, and it's even more valuable than *Man With Gazelle* would be."

I was thinking, of course, of Ernie Winston's messy watercolor portrait of Jeffrey upstairs. The "Boone" name I stole from the Conan Doyle story I was reading, Boone being the dude with the unfortunate lip. Ernie Boone didn't sound much like an artist's name to me, but I was thinking on the fly, and it's hard to come up with a good artist-type name when a gun is pointed at your forehead.

I could only see Howard's eyes, of course, but they were enough to tell me I'd scored a bull's-eye. I'm sure he smiled under his ski mask. "Tie those two up," he told Brandon, indicating Tony and Kendrick. "This one's gonna take us to the Boone painting."

Brandon got two chairs and put them back to back and had Kendrick and Tony sit in them. He made quick work of it, tied them securely to their seats and then, taking two handkerchiefs out of another jacket pocket, gagged them. Tony's eyes kept flashing over to me. He was frightened, naturally, but he seemed also to be trying to tell me to be careful. That's what I read from the look, anyway. When neither Brandon nor Howard was looking, I gave him a reassuring smile.

Howard tested the bonds holding Tony and Kendrick. Finding them satisfactory, he nodded to me. "Okay, hotshot. You're going to lead us to this other painting." He came over to me and grabbed my arm, poking the gun into the small of my back. "Now!"

We left the library and went up the stairs. Outside, the storm was still raging, rain lashing against the windows and thunder pealing periodically. As we got to the landing, lightning lit up the staircase. I hoped someone would hear us trudging up the steps and come out into the hall to investigate, but the sounds of the storm drowned out any noise we were making. When we got to the second floor, I glanced down the hall hopefully, but there was no sign of anyone stirring.

"It's in the tower," I said. "We have to go down the hall to the spiral staircase. It's the only way to get up there. Probably why Winston used that room to store his painting."

Howard paused, obviously not liking us having to walk past all the bedrooms. "Okay," he said, "but if you make a sound I'll shoot you and anyone stupid enough to poke their noses out into the hall. So walk slowly and carefully."

I did. Brandon stayed to my right side, and Howard was close behind me. His gun never shifted from the small of my back. I led them quietly down the hall to the stairs leading up to the nursery, my mind racing. I was trying to think of some way to get them to go into the nursery before me so that I could lock them in. Nothing was coming to me. I could only hope something would occur to me before Howard saw that the supposed valuable Boone was in fact a bad watercolor done by a snotty twelve-year-old.

We started up the winding steps. Howard's gun stayed against my spine. Not good. I could only hope that one of the Winston Manor spirits would make an appearance soon. It seemed a good night for the Gray Lady or Grandpa Winston to show themselves, and I was sure the sight of Specter Winston with half his face blown off would cause the brothers Smothers to flee and forget paintings and, more importantly, me.

The ghosts, drat their souls, utterly failed to appear. We reached the top of the steps and Howard and Brandon waited as I opened the door. I shielded the knob with my body so they wouldn't notice me pocketing the key. Swinging the door wide, I motioned for them to enter. "After you," I said.

With no window close to let in any light, I could barely make out their shadowy forms, but Howard prodded me with the gun. "Hardly. Get in there."

I entered, closely followed by the Smothers brothers. Howard growled for me to switch on a light, so I did, making sure I just hit one of the switches. One lamp hanging from the ceiling near the center of the room came on. The single bulb tried its best, but with the storm outside, it didn't illuminate much. Most of the room was in shadow, and the now broken bed to the side just looked like something from *The Cabinet of Dr. Caligari*. I shut the door behind us and, my hands behind my back, surreptitiously inserted the key into the lock, hoping that it wouldn't make any scratching sound. It did, but the brothers, intent on looking around the room for treasure, didn't seem to notice. I slid the key into my back pocket.

Howard gave me a shove, propelling me toward the center of the room. "Where's this painting? This don't look like no room you'd keep a painting in."

"Winston was just storing it up here." I could only hope these two were stupid enough to believe such a lame tale. "He was going to move it tomorrow to where the fake Zopfi is hanging now."

Howard's eyes darted about. "Where is it?"

Brandon stood guard near the door, exactly where I didn't want him to be. Even if I could find a moment when Howard's gun wasn't pointing at some vital spot on my body, I could hardly charge the door without his brother plugging me. It seemed I was sunk.

"It's over there, on the wall," I said with little enthusiasm. I pointed to Ernie's watercolor.

I saw Howard's eyes narrow as he moved to get a closer look. "What, this?" He was so surprised that he turned away from me, the gun lowering to his side.

I knew this could be my only chance. So I moved quickly. I admit I didn't think. If I thought, I wouldn't have moved. So I just moved.

First I balled my right hand into a fist and jumped and swung at the same time. The single bulb lighting the room shattered, plunging the room into darkness. I landed neatly and didn't pause to listen to the shuffling sounds from the brothers. Howard shouted, "What the fuck?" and Brandon fired his gun. The sound was deafening in the relatively small space. I felt nothing, so either he missed entirely or I was from Krypton. I moved toward the only patch of light—and that wasn't much—in the room, and that was the window. As I moved, I tore off my T-shirt.

Of course, moving toward the window meant they might be able to see my dark form blocking out the light, but I hoped they were too stunned by the sudden darkness to adjust quickly. One of them fired and this time I heard the bullet hit the wall near the window. There was more shuffling behind me, sounding like one of the brothers was trying to stop me.

I threw the window open and leaped onto the sill just as another shot rang out. There was a grunt and something heavy—I hoped it was a gun—hit the floor as Howard snarled, "Dumbass! You just shot me, you idiot!"

A bolt of lightning showed me where the broken pipe was. I wrapped my T-shirt around it as a sort of sling and jumped. The T-shirt helped to slow my descent enough that I wouldn't—hopefully—break both my legs when I hit bottom. The drainpipe was pretty weak from the damage Caps and I had already done to it, and I heard it groaning in protest. It bent away from the house a little more as I plummeted down. Not out to the side, so I wouldn't be able to hit the pool, but it did mean the Smothers brothers couldn't use it to get out of the room.

I haven't done much rock climbing, so what I did was more instinct than anything else. Gripping the ends of my T-shirt with both hands, I kept myself from sliding down too fast. Plus, as best I could, I wrapped my feet around the pipe. I was pelted with wind and rain, which was cold on my bare skin, but it was better than being in a room with two men with guns, even if they were imbeciles.

I hit the ground with a jolt, much harder and much sooner than I anticipated. Without being able to prepare for it, I let out a howl as a shock wave swept through me, and I fell backward, hitting the cement of the patio. Instinct kept my head up, so at least I didn't conk my noggin. I lay there, the breath knocked out of me, for several moments, wondering if I could move if I had to.

Looking up, I saw a whitish face appear in the nursery window. I don't know if it was Brandon or Howard, but whoever it was must have taken off his ski mask. A shot rang out. I heard the bullet hit somewhere close by, striking the cement. I rolled and tried to stand. My left leg didn't want to support my weight, and I went down again, scraping my hands on the cement as I tried to right myself. This time I got to my feet successfully, and I ran to the side door.

Behind me, I could hear the Smothers brothers shouting. One of them actually yelled, "Come back here!" That made me smile as I yanked open the side door and stumbled into the warmth of the house.

Chapter Eighteen

I UNTIED Tony first, of course. And then we made Kendrick wait as we hugged and kissed.

"Are you hurt?" Tony anxiously inquired.

Kendrick tried to say something, but the gag made his words hard to make out. I'm sure it was "You guys go ahead, I'm okay here for now."

"I'm fine. The knuckleheads are locked up in the nursery." I planted another kiss on Tony's lips. "You call 911. I'll untie Kendrick."

The next hour or two were pretty much pandemonium piled upon pandemonium. The shots had aroused the household, and soon everyone was either in the hall or the library, demanding explanations. I gave them the *Reader's Digest* condensed version of the events, promising to fill in the gaps later. Several of the bigger and braver of the Winston relatives volunteered to go up and guard the captive Smothers brothers. I later learned the goons had used up all their ammunition firing at me, so they couldn't even attempt to shoot the lock off the door.

Tony seemed glued to my side, and he and I both would let out an inappropriate laugh every now and then. After a crisis, I think the brain does that as a release. Winston, realizing his precious Zopfi had been in danger, paced around and asked questions to which I paid no attention. Ericka Winston moved from place to place, barking out sentences, demanding explanations. By the door, holding Jeffrey in his cage, Ernie merely looked disappointed that he'd missed all the fun. It actually seemed to me that there were more Winston relatives than I'd seen all weekend, like they'd multiplied overnight.

Among the crowd was Cecily, wearing either a nightgown of white with large black splotches on it or a clown suit, I'm not sure which. She scanned the throng until she latched her eyes onto me. With a squeal she ran up to me.

"Oh, you poor lamb! Are you hurt?"

"Nope. Lost some skin on my hands and a bruise or two from going down that drainpipe, but otherwise I'm unscathed." I shivered. My T-shirt was still outside on the patio, so I was bare-chested and the room had a chill to it, but I'm pretty sure the shivers were caused by her proximity.

She threw her arms around me and put her head against my breast. "You're so fantastic! I can't believe that you… why are you holding that young man's hand?"

"Oh, that. He's my boyfriend."

She blinked. "I don't understand."

I patted her head with my free hand. "I'm gay, Cecily."

"Oh, yeah. I knew that."

"You did? And you still want to marry me?"

"Of course!"

I was a bit flummoxed. Two goons with guns, easy. One loony fiancée, not so easy. "Really? I mean, what's in it for you? It's not like I'm rich or anything. All the money is in trust funds and stuff. I only get an allowance. Why would you want to marry me, knowing I'm gay?"

Her face scrunched up a bit as she thought about her answer. "You're cute."

"True, but there are others just as cute, if not more so, out there. Ones that like to sleep with women. Why not get your hooks into one of them?"

Her lips curled into a pout. "But I want you!" She even stomped her foot like a little kid. "I've always wanted you, ever since I first met you! I want to have babies with you!"

I'm afraid I couldn't stop my face from showing revulsion. "Well, *that* won't be happening!" Realizing I was being harsh with the insane young writer, I softened my look and gave her a pitying smile.

"What do you mean?" Her face was pretty empty. So were her eyes, and, I suspect, her brain.

"I don't have sex with women. Ever. So that won't be happening."

It took a moment, but something finally came into her eyes. Anger. She reached up and slapped my face. "In that case," she said hotly, "it's over!" She spun about and, shoving several assorted Winstons out of her way, stormed out of the room.

I looked at Tony. "Was it something I said?"

"May have been."

"She confuses me."

"I can understand that."

"I would have thought the being gay part would have done it. Maybe she thinks being gay is just a political statement." I slipped an arm around Tony because he looked like he needed it, not even thinking that, among the crowd, was Jasper K. Dollings, my dear stepmonster.

He didn't notice at first, having gone over to the telephone to call the police, even though I'd already told him that Tony had called them. He hung up and stood there in his pale blue pajamas, biting his lip, and finally glanced over at me.

"What are you doing," he thundered, "with your arm around that young man?"

I was feeling fairly euphoric. I'm sure Superman and Spider-Man, having vanquished Lex Luthor and the Green Goblin respectively, have the same feeling, like the world's a party and everyone is invited. I pulled Tony in close and gave him a peck on the cheek. "This," I announced proudly, "is my new boyfriend, Tony. Tony, I think you've already met my stepfather as you spooned peas onto his plate, but we'll make it official. Tony, this is Jasper K. Dollings."

Politely, but perhaps foolishly, Tony smiled and held out his hand for the stepmonster to shake. I braced myself, because there was the possibility Dollings would use it to yank Tony away from my side. "Pleased to meet you, sir," Tony said.

Dollings ignored both statement and proffered hand. He glared at me, his face so flushed I feared he might explode, and that would be one hell of a mess to clean up. "I would thank you," he told me, grinding his teeth, "to take your hands off that man! There are people watching!"

I looked around. "And it's odd. None of them seem to care, except you."

"I'm asking you for the last time to take your hands off him. I will not have a… fairy… for a stepson!" He emphasized the fairy part, like it was choking his throat just to say the word. I could only wish.

I nuzzled Tony's hair and kissed the top of his ear. I must have found one of his sensitive spots because I felt him shudder pleasurably. I'd have to remember that for later. Ear. G-spot. Resting the side of my head against Tony's cheek, I smiled at the stepmonster. "In that case," I said, "you'd better divorce my mother, because I am quite definitely of the fairy variety."

The muscles on Daddy Dollings's face were dancing, and the veins in his neck were doing their stretching exercises. "I can make life very difficult for you," he threatened.

"Yeah, I'm sure you could," I said easily, "for a while, at least. And then you'll go too far, and my mother will rebel and tell you where to get off. And even if she doesn't, I've decided I don't give a shit." I nuzzled Tony some more. Yep, that ear thing was going to come in handy. He giggled nervously as I gently bit his earlobe.

"You can kiss that car good-bye!" Dollings yelled.

"I hear they have this thing called public transportation. I might give that a try."

The stepmonster came up to me. I guessed he thought close proximity would result in me being frightened by him. It didn't work. "You'll regret this," he hissed.

"Doubt it," I replied, although my words were addressed to his back, as Dollings had turned to leave the room. With him gone, I returned my attention to Tony's lips. He kissed back but pulled away quickly.

"I'm sorry," he said. "I didn't mean to cause a problem."

"The problem is him, not you. And it was time for him to find out. Don't give the old goat a second thought."

I wanted to check on Caps, so Tony and I went out into the hall, where my buddy was still stretched out on the floor. His head was raised and he was propped up on his elbows. A concerned-looking Sutton was kneeling next to him.

"Honestly, I'm fine," Caps was saying. "I've taken much harder knocks than that. There was this time when Weasel and I were white-water rafting and—"

"You've got a concussion," Sutton said as he tried to get Caps to lie back down. "Now, just relax. I've called for an ambulance. It'll be here soon."

"But I don't need an ambulance!" Caps protested. "Really! I'm fine! I just got knocked out for a bit, which seems to happen a lot when I spend any amount of time with Weasel!" He noticed Tony and I were in attendance. "Tell him I'm fine, Weasel!"

I shook my head sadly. "I think he's a little delirious. Needs a lot of looking after, this one."

Caps sputtered. "What are you saying? I'm fine!"

Sutton's face was full of tenderness. "Please, I don't want you to get excited." He noted that several Winston relatives were hovering around. "Excuse me, could everyone stand back? We need a little air here!"

"But I'm fine!"

I clicked my tongue, making sympathetic noises. "You'd better lie down," I said to him, giving Caps a wink that went unnoticed by Sutton. To Sutton I said, "I'm worried. Was he saying something about white-water rafting? Must have been one hell of a knock. We've never been. Could he be brain-damaged, do you think?"

Sutton flashed me an angry glare. "You keep away from him! It seems like whenever you're around, Jake here ends up getting hurt! He's been hit, dunked in cold water several times, and tumbled down the stairs! And that's just this weekend! You're a menace!"

I thought that was a bit thick, but I was willing to take one for the team. I put on my best sad face. "Well, I was wanting to go with him in the ambulance to make sure he's all right—"

"I'm fine!" Caps insisted.

"Nothing doing!" Sutton said. "I'll go with him. If you were to ride with him, I'm sure you'd find some way to drop a fire extinguisher on his head or cause the ambulance to crash! I'll look after him."

Caps rolled his eyes. The poor sap just wasn't seeing his opportunity. "What is it going to take to convince you guys that I'm okay? Let me stand up, for Christ's sake!"

"Should his eyes be rolling back like that?" I asked. "Surely that's not normal. I'd better stay with him, make sure he gets to a hospital all right."

Sutton was adamant. "You stay away from him!" He looked down at Caps's face. "I'll stay with you. I want to make sure you're safe. Let the doctors check you out."

Something finally clicked in Caps's brain. He sank back to the floor and somehow managed to look pale and helpless. "You'll look after me?"

Sutton smiled. "You bet. You've got to have someone look after you." He quickly glared at me. "Just as long as it's not this guy. He'll get you killed."

Caps fluttered his eyelids. I think he overdid it a bit, but Sutton didn't seem to catch on to the sham. "I just don't want to go to the hospital. They're so lonely." He acted like he wanted to say more but was too weak to continue.

Sutton leaned down and placed his lips against Caps's right eyelid, stopping the fluttering. "Hush now. I'll stay with you." When Caps made a show of protest, Sutton became firm. "Now, you just relax. I'm going to look after you. It's no bother. In fact, it's a pleasure."

When Tony and I walked away, the two were holding hands. So were we. Tony seemed a little mystified. "What was that all about?"

"That was about Caps getting his guy," I said with a shrug. "I should have figured that out earlier. Sutton is one of those guys that likes to look after his significant other. He likes being the caregiver. And, goodness knows, Caps needs a lot of care."

Of course, this didn't explain Sutton's wanting to be with me. Surely he didn't think I needed looking after! Assuming it was just a weird fluke, Tony and I found a quiet room to await the arrival of the police.

Once the police arrived, it was questions, questions, raised eyebrows, and more questions. The two miscreants were carted off, as was Caps, although in a separate, more ambulance-y vehicle. True to his word, Keith Sutton rode into town with Caps. The last view I had of them was Sutton sitting by Caps's gurney, holding his hand.

The local police force must not have had much to do, because after the Smothers brothers were taken to the hoosegow, we had to go over the whole thing again. When they were finally done, I had to tell the tale to Ernie, who refused to go back to bed without hearing about the burglars. With Ernie I spiced it up a bit, adding extra danger and derring-do. His summation was an admiring "Gosh!"

Tony, who by this time had heard the tale more times than *Cats* played in the Winter Garden Theater on Broadway, smiled indulgently as I finished entertaining the young squirt. "If you're done bragging—"

"Just relating the facts."

"—maybe we should pack up some stuff to take to Caps. They'll keep him overnight at least. I think that's common procedure with a head injury case."

I smooched his cheek. "Wise thinking. I need to get out of this house, anyway. It's big, but not so big that I won't eventually bump into Cecily Talbot or the stepmonster, and I'm not popular with either of them at the moment."

We hit the stairs and there ran into Freeman the lawyer and Mark Winston, who insisted on pumping my arm like he was filling a tire with air. "I can't thank you enough for saving my Zopfi," he said, finally releasing my hand.

"Actually, I've got another present for you," I said, reaching into my back pocket for the envelope I'd retrieved from the floor before the police had been called. He read the message from his late wife silently, his eyes growing wider and wider the more he read.

"But this means—"

"Yes."

"Then the original will is still the real will!"

"Yes."

The lawyer, hearing a legal word, suddenly decided to become part of the conversation. "What's all this about wills?"

Winston, who had apparently forgotten the man had been standing there, flushed guiltily. "Nothing, nothing. Just thinking how good it was that the thieves didn't get into the safe and steal Charlotte's will."

"Her copy may be there," Freeman said stuffily, "but I have my copy in my briefcase, so it wouldn't have mattered."

Winston's mouth fell open. "You have a copy of the will?"

"Of course."

"But... but... but," Winston said, giving his impression of a skipping record. He recovered. "But she gave you the combination to the safe several days before she died. I was there. I saw you write the combination down in your notebook."

"Well, yes," the lawyer replied. "But that had nothing to do with her will. She kept her collection of Elvis commemorative plates in the safe. She thought, after her death, you might want to take them out and display them somewhere prominent, as a memorial to her. Although why she kept the damned things in the safe in the first place is beyond me. She thought they'd be worth a fortune, I suspect."

"Are they?"

"Might be worth something to an Elvis collector. I can check into it, if you like."

Tony and I made our excuses, explaining that we were on a mission for Caps, and left the lawyer and Winston on the stairs chatting about plates and their relative value. At the top of the stairs, though, we encountered another roadblock, this time in the shape of Tyler Kendrick and Cecily Talbot. Kendrick was obviously in the middle of telling the author about the events of the night, playing up his own role. I didn't get to hear much, but apparently in his version he had a fistfight with the burglars, because he was in the middle of demonstrating his right-left-right combination when he caught sight of us. He paused his tale. Cecily, who'd been listening attentively, saw me and suddenly decided she wanted to be elsewhere. With a huff she spun on her heel and retreated down the hall. Kendrick, deprived of his audience, decided to be chummy with us, even going so far as to put an arm around us both.

"Some night, eh?" he said.

"It wasn't without its points of interest," I said, drawing on my cache of Sherlock Holmes quotes.

He laughed and slapped me on the back. "Hey, I should really tell your cousin about this. I bet she'd love to hear about what happened. You wouldn't want to give me her number, would you? I'm sure Kitty wouldn't mind."

I shook my head. "I have a policy not to give out numbers without permission. Sorry." I extricated myself from his grasp, and Tony and I started down the hall to Caps's room. I thought Kendrick would give up and slink away, but he followed us.

"Some night, huh?" he repeated as we entered Caps's room. The sun had risen, although it wasn't making much of a show, if the light coming in the window was anything to go by. It was going to be a gray, gloomy day, as far as the weather went, but I was still fairly chipper, even with Kendrick hovering around. Tony located Caps's suitcase, and together we found some clothes to throw into it.

"This isn't your room, is it?" Kendrick asked.

"No," I told him. "We're getting some stuff together to take to Caps."

"Is he okay?" Kendrick did his best to sound interested.

"I'm sure he's got a lump on his noggin and one hell of a headache, but he seemed to be doing well when they hauled him away." I added some extra underwear to the suitcase, just in case.

Nothing worse than running out of underwear. I found his car keys on top of his dresser and slipped them into my pocket. As I'd come with him, I figured Caps wouldn't object to my using his car to bring him the necessities of life.

"He'll need his toothbrush," Tony said, disappearing into the bathroom. Once there, he let out an exclamation. "Hey! You'll never believe what I found on the floor in here! A gray dress and a blonde wig! You never told me that Caps did drag."

Tony came out of the bathroom holding the wig. He shook it out and examined it carefully before looking at me mischievously. "It's not a bad wig. Wonder what you'd look like—"

And before I could stop him, he plopped the wig onto my head. I tried to shake it off, but he held it in place and tried to adjust it. "No, come on! You look cute with it on!"

Kendrick, however, wasn't finding my bewigged head cute. He frowned in thought, probably wondering why the sight of me with long tresses seemed familiar. And then realization dawned, and his eyes bugged out like Wile E. Coyote's just before the plunge off some precipice. "You!" he bellowed.

"Huh?" I asked, removing the headdress, hoping to play it off by pretending innocence.

"You! It was you!"

"What was?"

"Kitty! I… I kissed you!"

"Nonsense! Just family resemblance!"

Kendrick studied my face intently. "No, it was you! You tricked me into kissing you!" Further thoughts flooded into his excuse for a brain. "You crushed my balls!"

"Now, don't jump to conclusions—"

I didn't get any further. He didn't jump to conclusions. He jumped toward me, his hands balled into fists and murder in his eyes.

Tony was in between me and Kendrick, and it was only the fact that Kendrick had to pause to shove Tony aside that saved me from getting pummeled. I had to leap onto the bed and off the other side to get around Kendrick, who luckily for me was big but not fast. At the door I shot a smile in Tony's direction. "I'll call you!" I shouted before belting down the hall. Kendrick was close behind him.

It seemed that most of the household had elected to remain awake after the burglary, and they were still dotted about the premises. I felt many eyes on me as I ran down the stairs and made my way to the front door. Kendrick followed, but he was losing ground, mainly because he wasted his breath cursing me and telling me what he was going to do to me once he caught me. I didn't catch it all, but removing my arms and stuffing them down my throat was part of the agenda.

Before I got to the front door, I had to do a quick step around the stepmonster, who was standing around chatting with Mark Winston. At the sight of me running for dear life, he sputtered, "What's going on? What are you doing now?"

"Leaving!" I shouted as I threw open the door and ran out onto the front lawn. I got to Caps's car and had started the engine before Kendrick even made it to the driveway. I had to maneuver the car around him while he stood, shaking his fist at me and bellowing something about stomping on my spleen. I pushed the gas pedal down and burned rubber down the drive, leaving Kendrick panting and still yelling his threats.

All in all, it had been an interesting weekend.

Chapter Nineteen

THE protesters were out in front of the 21 Club in force. I spotted several familiar faces, such as the woman with the Gorgon hair, but the stepmonster was not among them.

It had been five days since the Winston Manor affair (or as Caps referred to it, the weekend from Hell), and so far I'd managed not to run into dear old Dollings. I'd heard a lot secondhand, through my mother, and I knew I wasn't on his favorites list.

I sauntered past the protesters, hands stuffed into the pockets of my hoodie. I was perfectly happy to let them yell at me as I strode toward the entrance to the club, but the Gorgon woman decided she wanted to get right up in my face and scream at me.

"You're walking straight into Hell!" Her face was red with emotion.

"Been there already," I told her with a smile. "And, really, do something about that hair. It's atrocious!"

"There's no need to get personal," was her comeback.

"Honey, you're telling me how I should live my life. How much more personal can you get?"

I left her to ponder that and went inside the club. Once again the doorman examined my ID carefully, handing it back to me with an indulgent smile. "You can go in," he said, like he was letting me get away with murder.

"I really am twenty-one, you know," I told him.

"And I'm Chuck Norris."

I shrugged. There was no convincing some people.

The 21 Club was hopping that night. On the main stage, several drag queens were recreating the "Mein Herr" number from *Cabaret*, complete with wooden chairs to slump over and torn fishnet stockings. The crowd was hooting and hollering. I can't say I blame them. Although I'd come in at the end of the routine, I could see the girls had worked hard on the number, especially the six-foot-four Liza clone. The song ended, and the queens went to the edge of the stage to quickly snap up the dollar bills being waved at them by the hungry horde.

I looked around for familiar faces. I knew Caps was at one of the tables, as he'd texted me only minutes before, complaining that Keith Sutton wouldn't allow him to drink, it being too soon after his concussion. I couldn't see him. I did, however, spot the club manager seated at his usual table. The bastard had the nerve to smile and nod at me, which I thought was a bit ballsy after he had forced me to resort to drag to escape his club unnoticed. As I was in a forgiving mood, though, I smiled and nodded back.

The announcer informed the throng that the next performer was Daisy Day, and a buxom Dolly Parton-ish queen came onto the stage and began strutting her stuff as the speakers thumped out "9 To 5." The audience clapped in time to the music.

I forced my way through the crowd. The place was packed. Every table was taken, and the dance floor was pretty much filled with boys. I craned my neck to check out the tables across the way and spotted Caps and Sutton. I waved. They waved back. To get to them, I'd have to machete my way through a few hundred sweaty party boys, so I mouthed *I'll catch up with you later.* Caps didn't catch it, so I had to mouth the words again. I don't know if he understood, but he nodded as if he did and then returned to gazing adoringly into Sutton's eyes. Sutton, who either hadn't spotted me or preferred not to acknowledge me right then, stroked Caps's cheek gently before leaning over to kiss my friend's lips. Something told me they didn't need me around anyway.

"Well, if it isn't Mr. Weasel," said a voice behind me.

I turned to find Zach—or more precisely, Kitty Mews, as he was in full drag—standing there, martini in hand. "Hello, Kitty," I said.

He placed a hand on my shoulder and got closer. "And how are you, tonight? Need another makeover? The protesters are out there again tonight."

"Nope. No need any longer. The stepfather knows I'm a homo now," I said.

"Was he terribly upset when he found out?"

"Apoplectic," I answered.

I was stating mere facts. The man was furious with me, I knew from some of the tidbits of his ire that were passed on to me by my mother. One of my favorites was when he told my mom that I'd have to join the Marines, because they'd "beat the queer out of me," as he put it. My mother, not wanting her baby to leave her for that long a period of time, put her foot down on that notion quickly. She did cave in on the car, though, and for two days I lost the Corvette. I got it back when I informed her that I'd missed every single one of my classes on Monday and Tuesday due to the inability of public transport to get me to Rockford College in a timely manner. They might have done so if I'd bothered to leave my apartment and go down to the bus stop, but I didn't point this out to my mom. In any case, the 'Vette was once again mine.

"I'm sure he'll get over it," Kitty said. He downed the rest of his martini and pressed against me, running his hand over my chest. "I don't normally go for the skinny ones, but you're kind of cute. I don't go on again until the next show. Why don't you and I head to the dressing room and get better acquainted?"

I gently removed his hand, which was tweaking my nipple though my T-shirt. "Sorry," I said, "but I'm meeting someone here."

Kitty didn't look too disappointed, although I did notice his eyes straying to my groin to check out that area. "Lucky boy," he said. "But if things don't work out, you know where to find me."

I grinned. "You'll be among the first to know," I assured him, not meaning a word of it. And, of course, Kitty knew I didn't. He flirted out of habit and would have been surprised if I'd taken him up on his offer.

I heard someone scream my name and turned to see the twins, Donald and Darren, out on the dance floor, shirtless and sweaty, bouncing to the Dolly Parton tune and trying to get Daisy's attention so they could tip her. Donald—maybe it was Darren—had spotted me and was waving like a madman. I waved back. Again, it would take many precious minutes to push my way through the crowd to get to them, and it wasn't them I was there to see. I did the universal Call You Later signal by putting an imaginary phone to my ear. Donald Maybe Darren smiled and returned to hooting at the drag show.

I fought my way to the side bar, which was busy but at least not as manic as the main bar. There I found Horrible Harry in residence, it apparently being Dave the Barman's night off. Harry was leaning across the bar, trying to flirt with a customer.

I say "trying" because I could see he was getting nowhere. That made me smile, as his customer was Tony. As I approached, I could hear Tony telling him, "Sorry, I've got a boyfriend. At least, I think he is."

I came up quietly and put my arms around him. "He is if you want him to be," I said before nibbling his ear. The nibbling caused Tony to squirm pleasurably, and he let out a little giggle.

"You're late," he said as I released him to sit on the bar stool next to him. Harry, conceding defeat, stopped leaning to gaze into

Tony's eyes and asked me what I wanted to drink. I ordered a vodka and tonic and then promptly forgot that Harry or anyone else in the bar existed. I turned to look at Tony's beautiful face.

"I know. I often am. It's something you'll have to get used to if we're going to be an item."

Tony grinned. "I have the terrible feeling that there's going to be a lot I'm going to have to get used to."

"Possibly true," I admitted.

Tony set down the bottle of beer he'd been holding and grabbed hold of my hand. His fingers were slightly damp and chilly from the brew, but I barely noticed. I was too busy enjoying the electricity that shot down my arm from his mere touch. "So," he said, "how bad has it been at home?"

I shrugged. "I haven't been to my parents' house yet. Been sticking to the apartment. I'm sure I'll brave going back sometime about, oh, let's say next July."

"Did your stepfather take away your car?"

"He tried, but as you know weasels are known for their ingenuity. I got it back the other day."

"Well, that's good. And your friend Jake?"

"He's in the main room as we speak, with his new boyfriend, Sutton."

"Well, that's good."

"We'll see if it lasts. They're happy for now, and that's the important thing. I'm afraid, though, that Sutton isn't the most reliable guy to date. Still, time will tell."

"It always does." Tony paused to order another beer as Harry set my vodka and tonic down in front of me. Harry darted an evil glance at me (like he had a chance with Tony in any case!) and went off again. Tony squeezed my hand. "At least you're not engaged any longer."

"That was weird."

"Cecily is weird. Is she still publishing her book with your stepfather's publishing company?"

"No, she pulled out. Another reason for the stepmonster to be furious with me. You can't win them all, though. You'd think he'd be happy. After all, any gal that desperate to get married can't be a good client to have in your ranks. She'd want all sorts of odd things written into her contract, like only having green M&Ms at book signings and having Chippendale dancers on hand to open the books to the correct page for her to autograph. I feel sorry for the next poor sod she gets her claws into. Hopefully the next one will at least be straight."

"It will help if he's as loony as she is."

"True."

There was a short pause before Tony said, "I want to be honest with you."

"Feel free."

"You scare the hell out of me."

"I have that effect on people."

"And it's not just the robbery, the sliding down drainpipes, and the being tied up. It's you."

"Me?"

"I have the feeling that you're dangerous to be around. That things just seem to explode when you're around, or tarantulas crawl out from under beds, or ocean liners sink. I think you're one of those people that are danger magnets."

"I don't mean to be."

"I know. Still, it frightens me. I'm kind of a simple guy. I live in a small town, where nothing happens. I mean, in Shannon it's big news when a cat gets stuck up a tree. You, on the other hand, ran out of the house because a huge gardener was chasing you, wanting to rip you limb from limb."

"He's only a gardener on his off hours. Normally he's a policeman."

"Don't split hairs. You know what I mean. Have you seen him since?"

"No, and I hope to put off reacquainting myself with Tyler Kendrick for a couple of years at least. He's about the size of an elephant, and like that beast, Kendrick never forgets."

Tony shook his head sadly. "That's just what I'm saying. What's your middle name?"

"Believe it or not, it's Carrington."

"Your parents missed out there. They should have named you Trouble."

I began to get that cold feeling in the pit of my stomach. "What are you saying? That you don't want to date me?"

Tony smiled and shook his head. "That's the trouble! I can't get you out of my mind. I don't care if people point guns at me or things explode, as long as I'm sure you'd be there by my side. And that's what scares me! It's so not me."

"I promise," I said, leaning in until our foreheads touched, "not to let anything explode around you. We'll live boring lives. I'll go to all my classes and graduate and make a name for myself in the business world, and you'll… what do you want to do?"

Tony kissed me, smiling. Well, our mouths were close, so it seemed like the thing to do. "Right now, Mark Winston's hired me on permanently at Winston Manor. So it's me, Mrs. Donleavey, and even Andrew working there full time. Now that he knows he'll have his wife's money to keep the house running, I guess he needed a regular staff."

"Good for you! Winston seems like he'd be a good boss."

"Not bad. Still, it means I'm far away from you."

"Not that far."

Tony lowered his voice so that Harry, hovering nearby, couldn't hear. "Something else bothers me."

"Tell all."

"I jumped right into bed with you! I'm not like that. I have a strict rule that I don't sleep with someone until after at least the third date, and I hopped right into bed with you after knowing you only minutes! Granted, the first time we were interrupted by your stepfather…." He let the sentence dangle.

"That was scary," I agreed.

"Not as scary as the effect you have on me."

I squeezed his hand. "What do you want me to do about it? Tell me, and I'll do it!"

Tony laughed. "Nothing. There's nothing you can do. You're you. You're a walking disaster area, but I think that's going to have to be another one of those things I'll have to try to get used to."

A nervous laugh came out of me. The way Tony had been talking, I thought we were having one of those I Like You But I Can't Date You talks. I was glad it turned out not to be the case. "Honestly," I said, "last weekend was a fluke. Normally my life is quiet."

"I don't believe you." Tony leaned into me. We only stayed on the barstools by holding onto each other and steadying ourselves. I kissed him. We separated clumsily, nearly upsetting both my drink and the fresh beer Henry had just put down in front of Tony. Once we made sure the drinks weren't going to topple over, we looked at each other guiltily.

"You can't blame that one entirely on me," I said.

"Maybe you're contagious."

"I'm sure there's some sort of inoculation you can get."

Tony laughed and cupped my face in his hands before carefully—mindful of the drinks—leaning in to kiss me.

"Weasel!"

The shout came from the doorway, and it had a curious echo to it. Tony and I turned, and I saw it had been two people calling out to me at once, giving my name the curious echo effect. In the door, side by side, were the Latino I'd danced with a week previously and McCaffrey, both of whom were glaring at me. At least, I'm assuming it was McCaffrey. With his head up and his eyes open, he looked different.

The two had apparently come into the side bar and spoken my name in tandem by total accident. Realizing they'd both called out my name, they looked at each other.

"Excuse me," the Latino said in heavily accented English, "but I need to speak to Weasel."

McCaffrey didn't seem impressed. "Well, take a number. I need to talk to him myself. My talk is more important, so you'll just have to wait."

"I beg your pardon," the Latino said, "but my talk is the more important. Weasel and I danced last week, and—"

"Yeah, well, Weasel and I did more than dance last week. At least, I think we did. I was too drunk to remember."

It seemed I was never to learn if McCaffrey and I engaged in coitus. Oh, well. Water under the bridge now.

The Latino wasn't going to shift his position. "I need to talk to Weasel. I dropped my wallet while we were dancing—"

"Dropping your wallet in this place is as good as losing it. You don't think Weasel paused to pick it up without—"

"I just want to ask Weasel if he—"

"Well, I want to ask Weasel if we—"

The Latino tried to move past McCaffrey to approach me. McCaffrey shoved him.

I don't know if you've even been in a bar when a fight has broken out, but there's an almost visible tension in the air right before the first punch is thrown. That tension was surrounding the two in the doorway, egging them on. Squaring his shoulders, the Latino glared at McCaffrey. "Did you just shove me?"

"I believe I did."

The tension erupted, and the Latino punched McCaffrey right on the nose. McCaffrey stumbled back, crashing into a guy at the bar who was in the process of taking a sip of his whiskey sour. The resulting jolt sent the drink all over his face. He turned to see who had hit him. "Hey!" he protested. He might have said more, but McCaffrey punched him in the face. I'm not sure he meant to. I think he was still in shock from the blow he'd taken from the Latino and was just lashing out, hoping he'd bop the Latino back.

The guy sitting next to the dude now wearing a whiskey sour seemed to think he was missing out on the fun, because he hauled himself off his stool and punched McCaffrey and then launched himself at the Latino.

Within minutes nearly everyone in the side bar had gotten into it, with punches being thrown, shins being kicked, and shouts and screams all around.

I pulled Tony off his stool and clutched him tightly. "We need to leave!" I shouted over the uproar.

"This is what I'm talking about!" Tony yelled back.

We ducked out of the way as the Latino and the whiskey sour guy picked up a now unconscious McCaffrey and tossed him over the bar. He hit lots of glasses and bottles on his way to the floor, making Henry scream in terror. I quickly glanced over the bar. McCaffrey was out of it, but other than his nose, he didn't seem to be bleeding, so the glass hadn't cut him. Some people from the main bar must have come over to see what all the noise was about, because suddenly the room was filled with people, most of whom were trying to hit each other. I pulled Tony over to the wall and, crouching, we slowly made our way to the door. When trying to leave a room where a bar fight has erupted, go along the side, never try to go through. Once the frenzy has hit, people don't care who they're slugging.

We made it to the exit unscathed. Once outdoors and away from the maddened crowd, Tony glared at me, although it was more a puzzled look than an angry one. "What was that all about?"

"I'm not sure. I danced with the one guy last week, and I may have slept with the other one, but as to why fists started flying—"

Tony laughed and grabbed me by the elbow, propelling me toward the parking lot. "Just like I said, you're a danger magnet! Let's get out of here. I think I hear sirens in the distance."

I didn't argue with him. With my luck, one of the police called to the scene would end up being Tyler Kendrick, and if so, I knew he'd find some reason to arrest me. Tony and I moved quickly past the protesters, who were clearly puzzled as to why police cars were coming down the street toward them. I saw several of them hiding their protest signs behind their backs.

Laughing, Tony and I went to my car and got inside. "We'll come back for your car in the morning," I said. "You can stay the night with me. That is, if you'd like."

"Oh, I'd like."

"We don't have to do anything you don't want to do."

Tony shrugged as he fastened his seat belt. "That won't leave much." He turned his face so I could see his grin.

"Good thing you're strapped in, then," I said as I gunned the engine.

STEPHEN OSBORNE has been an improvisational comedian, a pizza restaurant manager, and a bookseller. Other than writing, his addictions include British television shows, reading mysteries, and (a recent addition) Broadway musicals. He lives in rural Illinois with Jadzia the One-Eyed Wonder Dog.

Visit him at Facebook: http://facebook.com/stephen.osborne2 and Twitter: http://twitter.com/southbendghosts. You can contact him at leftyIN@yahoo.com.

Duncan Andrews thrillers from STEPHEN OSBORNE

Also from STEPHEN OSBORNE

STEPHEN OSBORNE

WRESTLING WITH JESUS

http://www.dreamspinnerpress.com